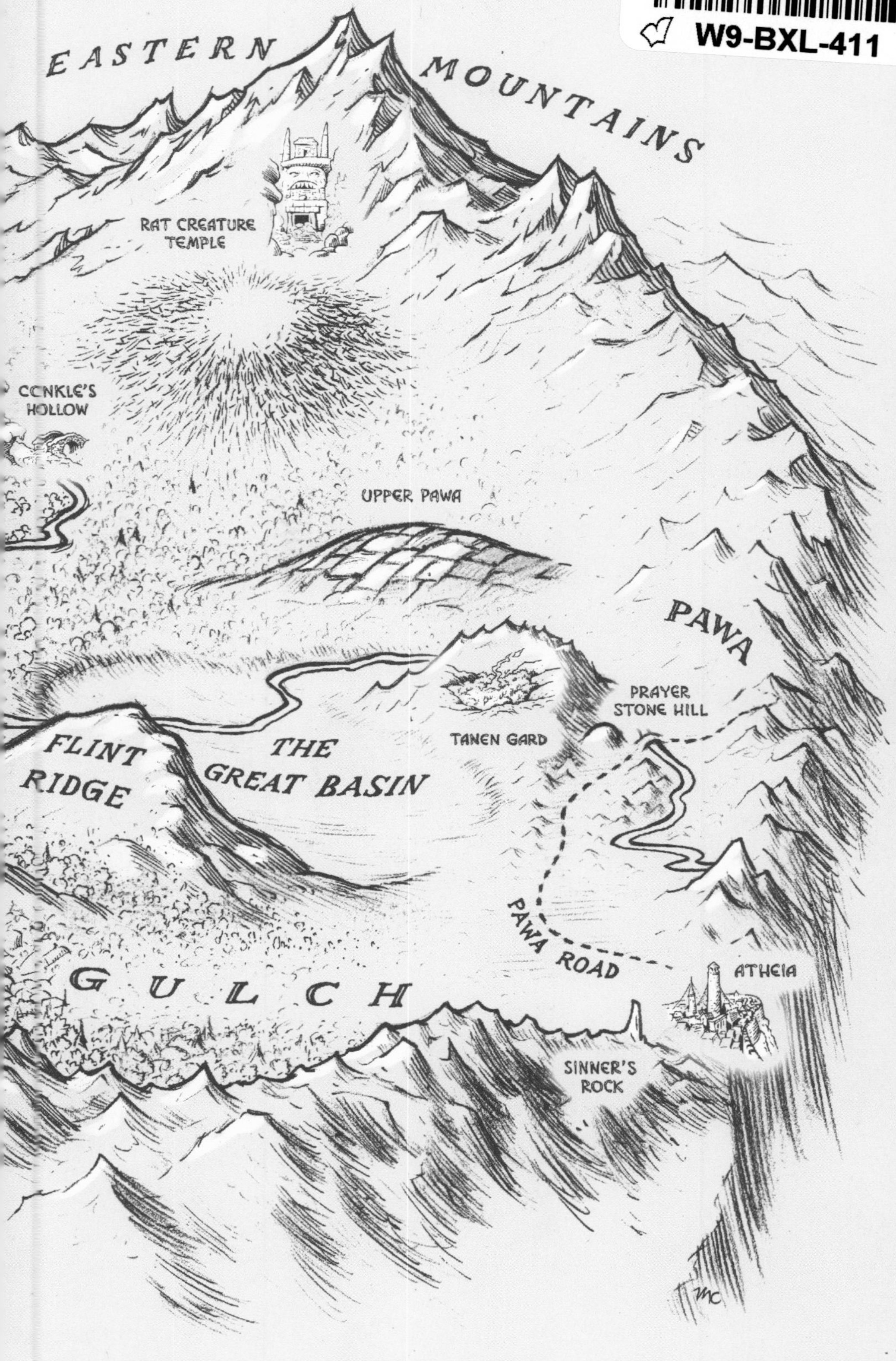
EASTERN MOUNTAINS
RAT CREATURE TEMPLE
CONKLE'S HOLLOW
UPPER PAWA
PAWA
PRAYER STONE HILL
TANEN GARD
FLINT RIDGE
THE GREAT BASIN
PAWA ROAD
ATHEIA
GULCH
SINNER'S ROCK
MC

Dreaming of Harvestar

BONE

Out from Boneville

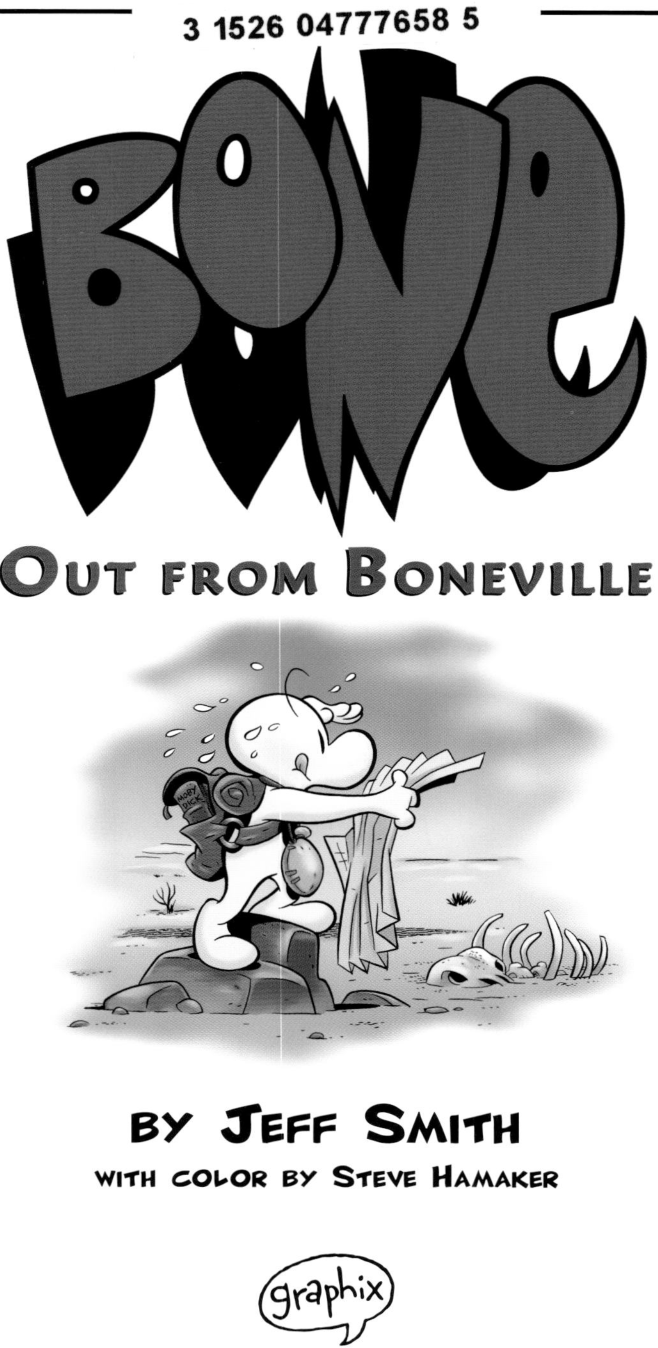
MOBY DICK

By Jeff Smith

with color by Steve Hamaker

graphix

An Imprint of

SCHOLASTIC

This book is for Vijaya

Copyright © 2005 by Jeff Smith.

The chapters in this book were originally published in the comic book BONE and are copyright © 1991 and 1992 by Jeff Smith. BONE® is copyright © 2005 by Jeff Smith.

Library of Congress Cataloging-in-Publication Data is available.

ISBN-13: 978-0-439-70623-0 – ISBN-10: 0-439-70623-8 (hardcover)

ISBN 0-439-70640-8 (paperback)

ACKNOWLEDGMENTS

Harvestar Family Crest designed by Charles Vess

Map of *The Valley* by Mark Crilley

20   19   18   15

First Scholastic edition, February 2005

Book design by David Saylor

Printed in Singapore 46

CONTENTS

- CHAPTER ONE -

THE MAP - - - - - - - - - - - - - - - - - 1

- CHAPTER TWO -

THORN - - - - - - - - - - - - - - - - 27

- CHAPTER THREE -

PHONEY BONE - - - - - - - - - - - - - 51

- CHAPTER FOUR -

KINGDOK - - - - - - - - - - - - - - - 73

- CHAPTER FIVE -

BARRELHAVEN - - - - - - - - - - - - - 95

- CHAPTER SIX -

PHONEY'S INFERNO - - - - - - - - - - 117

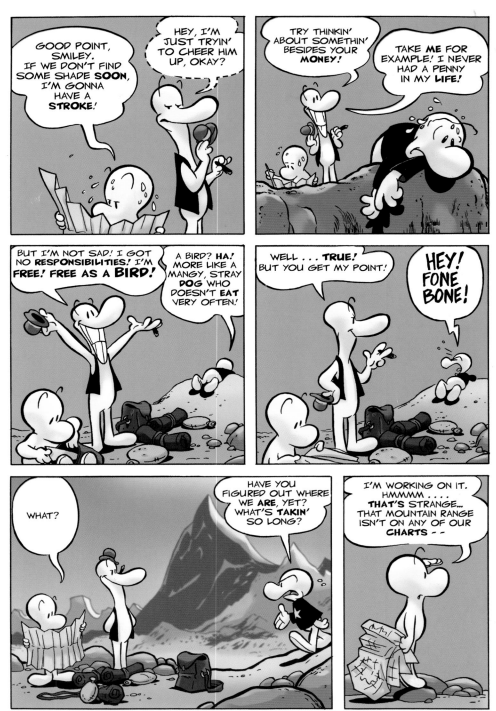

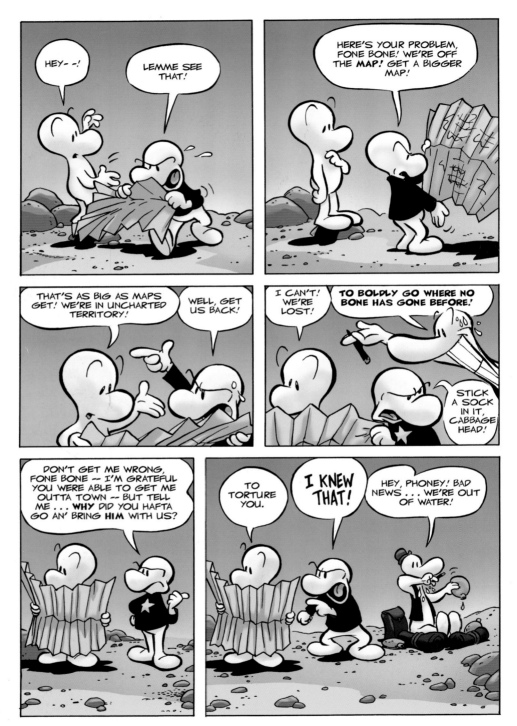

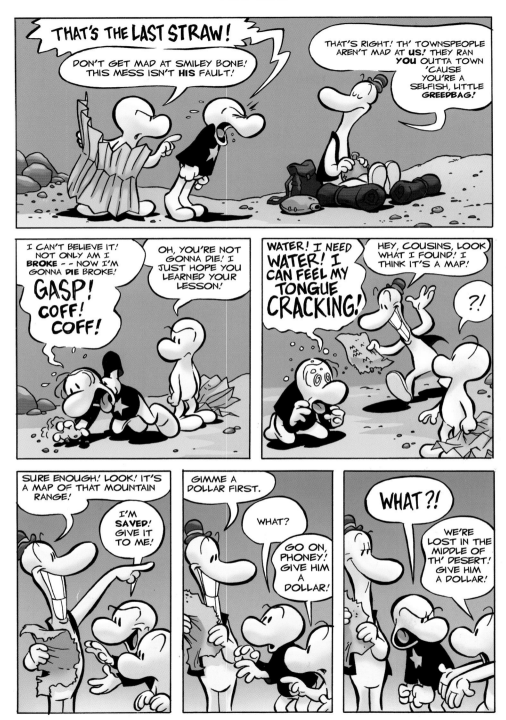

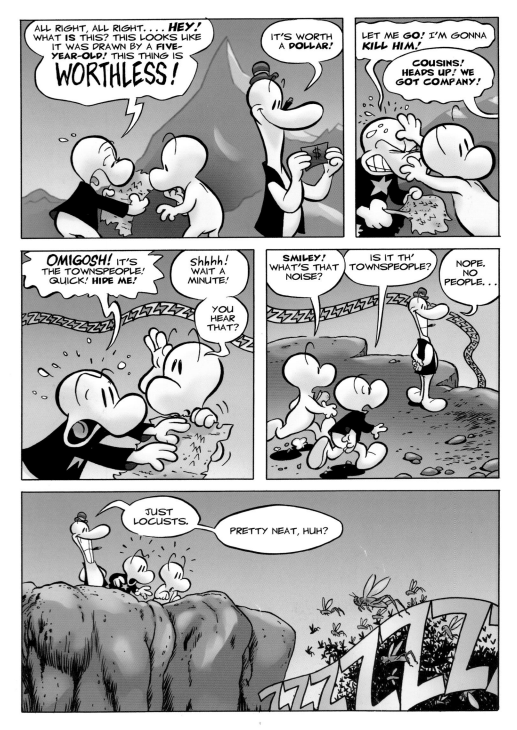

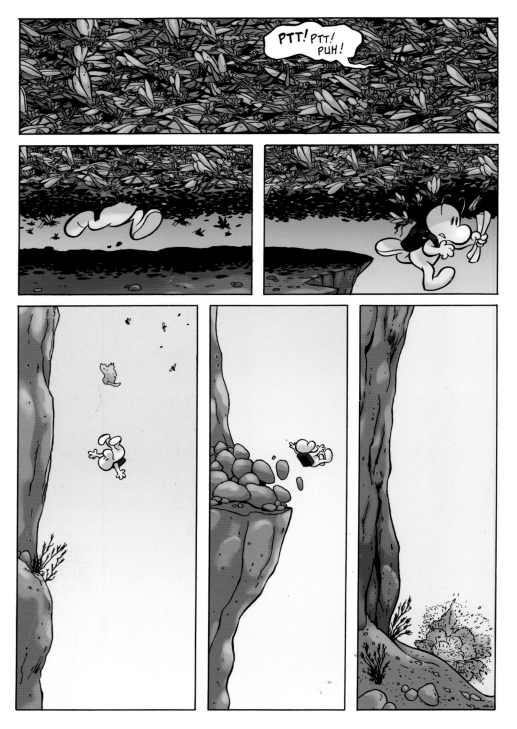

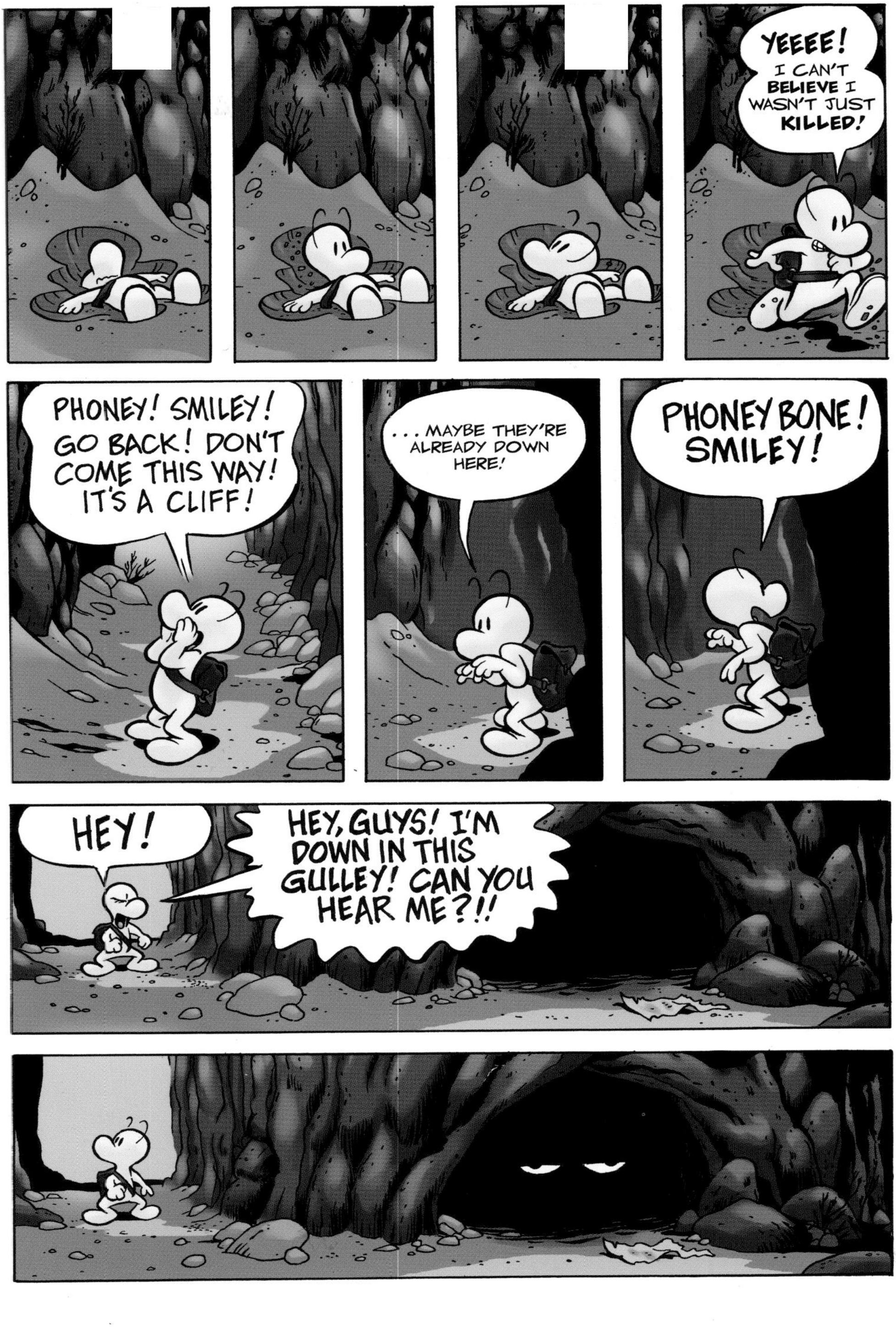
YEEEE!
I CAN'T BELIEVE I WASN'T JUST KILLED!
PHONEY! SMILEY! GO BACK! DON'T COME THIS WAY! IT'S A CLIFF!
...MAYBE THEY'RE ALREADY DOWN HERE!
PHONEY BONE! SMILEY!
HEY!
HEY, GUYS! I'M DOWN IN THIS GULLEY! CAN YOU HEAR ME?!!

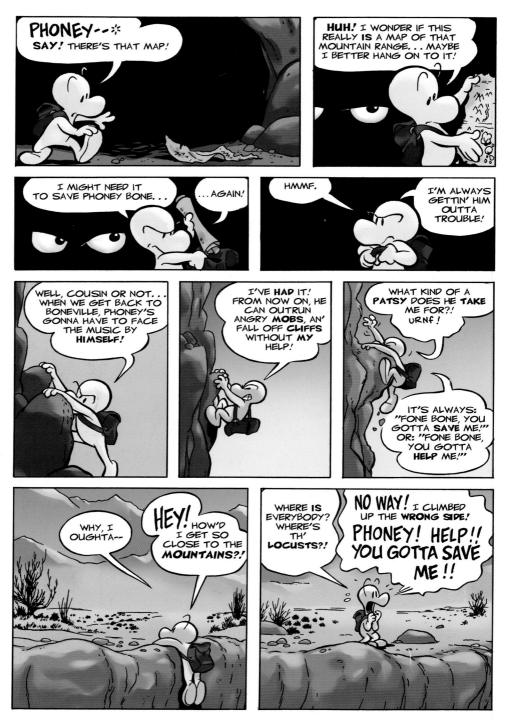

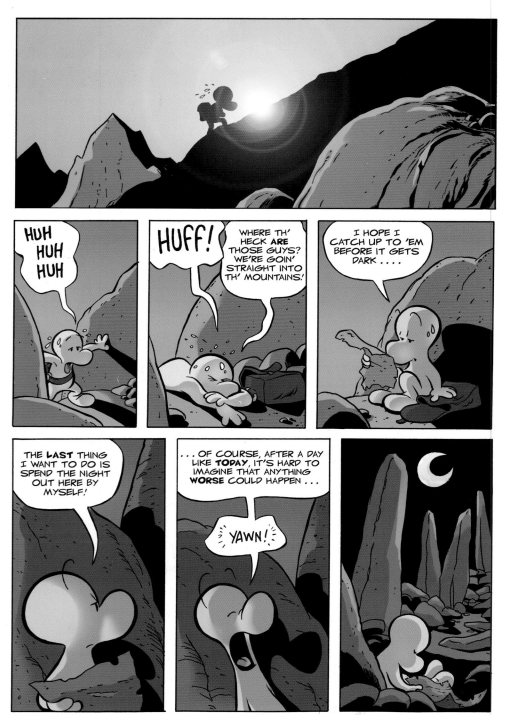

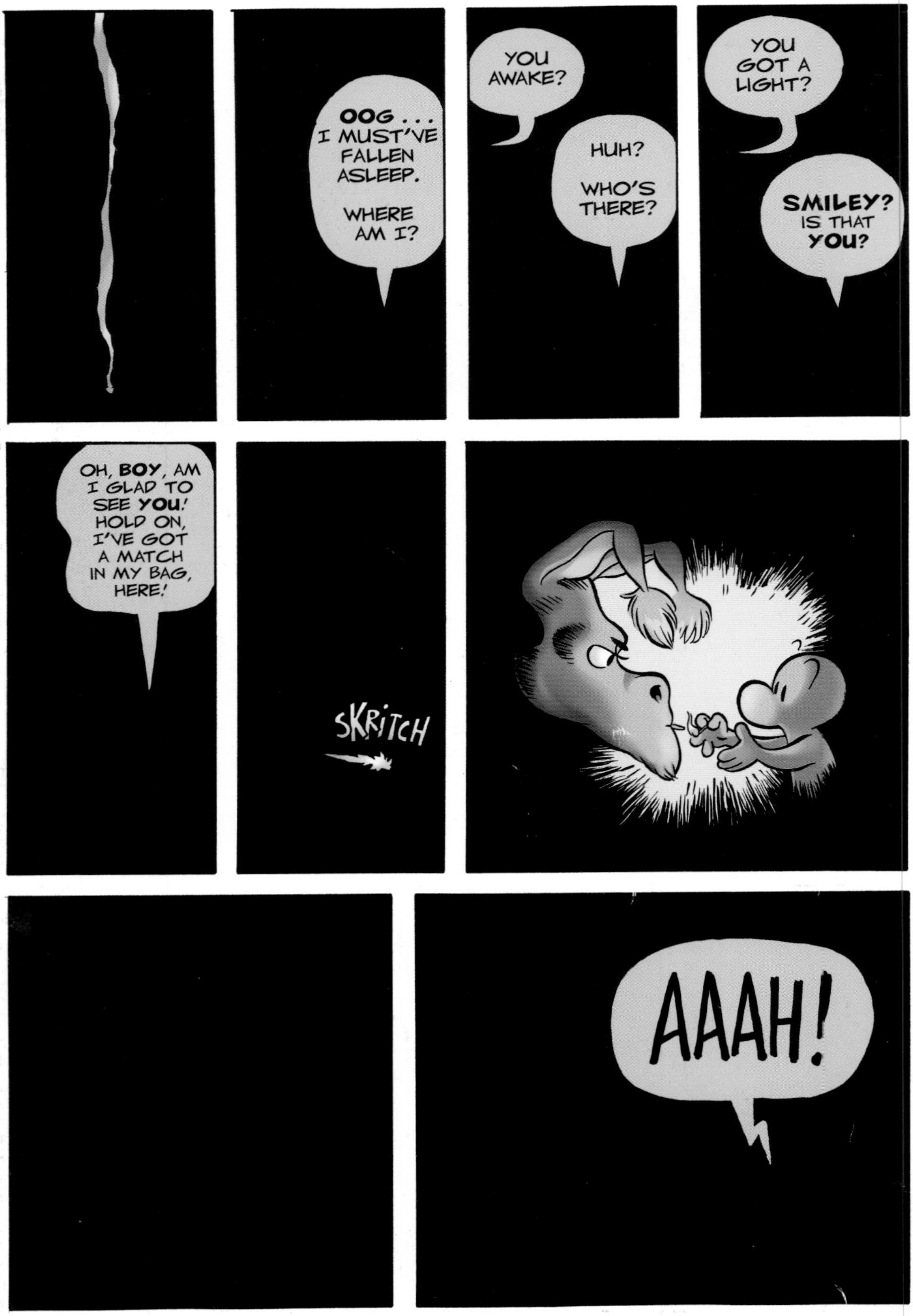
OOG . . . I MUST'VE FALLEN ASLEEP.
WHERE AM I?
YOU AWAKE?
HUH?
WHO'S THERE?
YOU GOT A LIGHT?
SMILEY? IS THAT YOU?
OH, BOY, AM I GLAD TO SEE YOU! HOLD ON, I'VE GOT A MATCH IN MY BAG, HERE!
SKRITCH
AAAH!

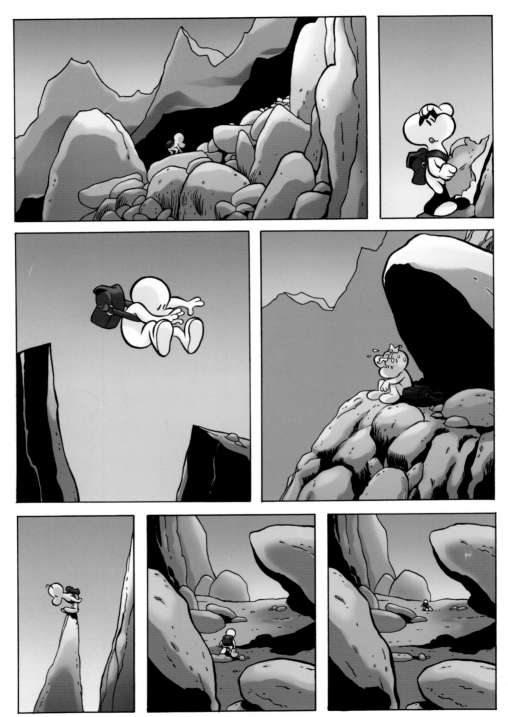

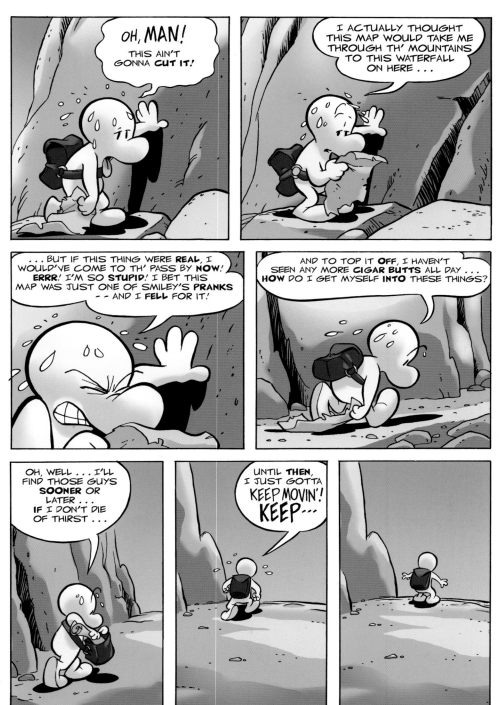

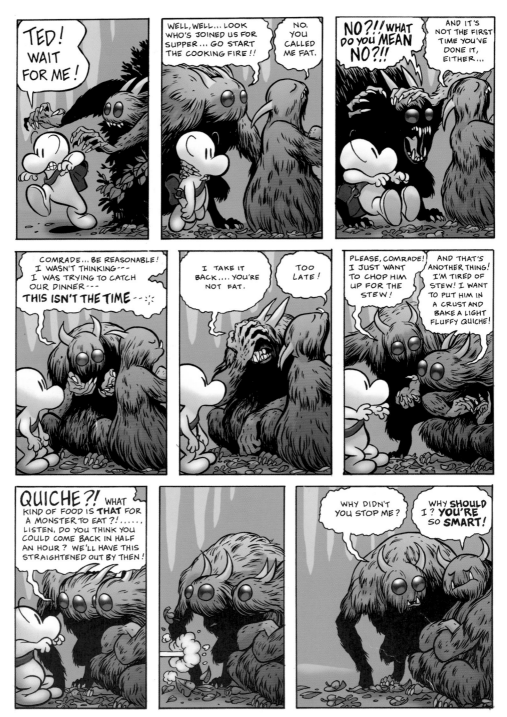

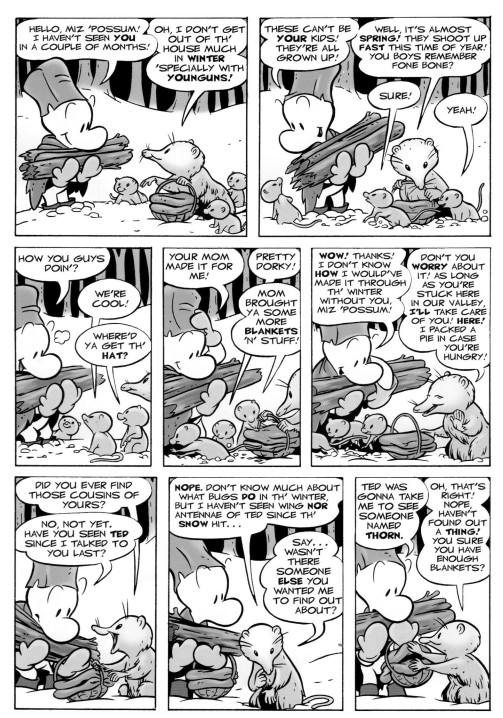

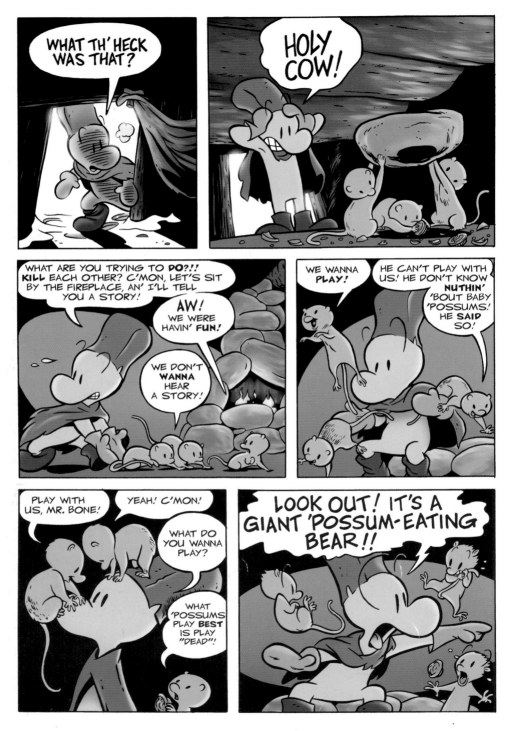

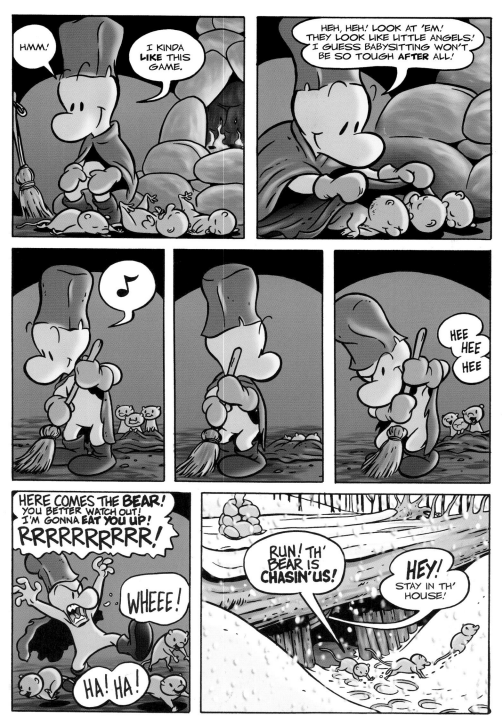

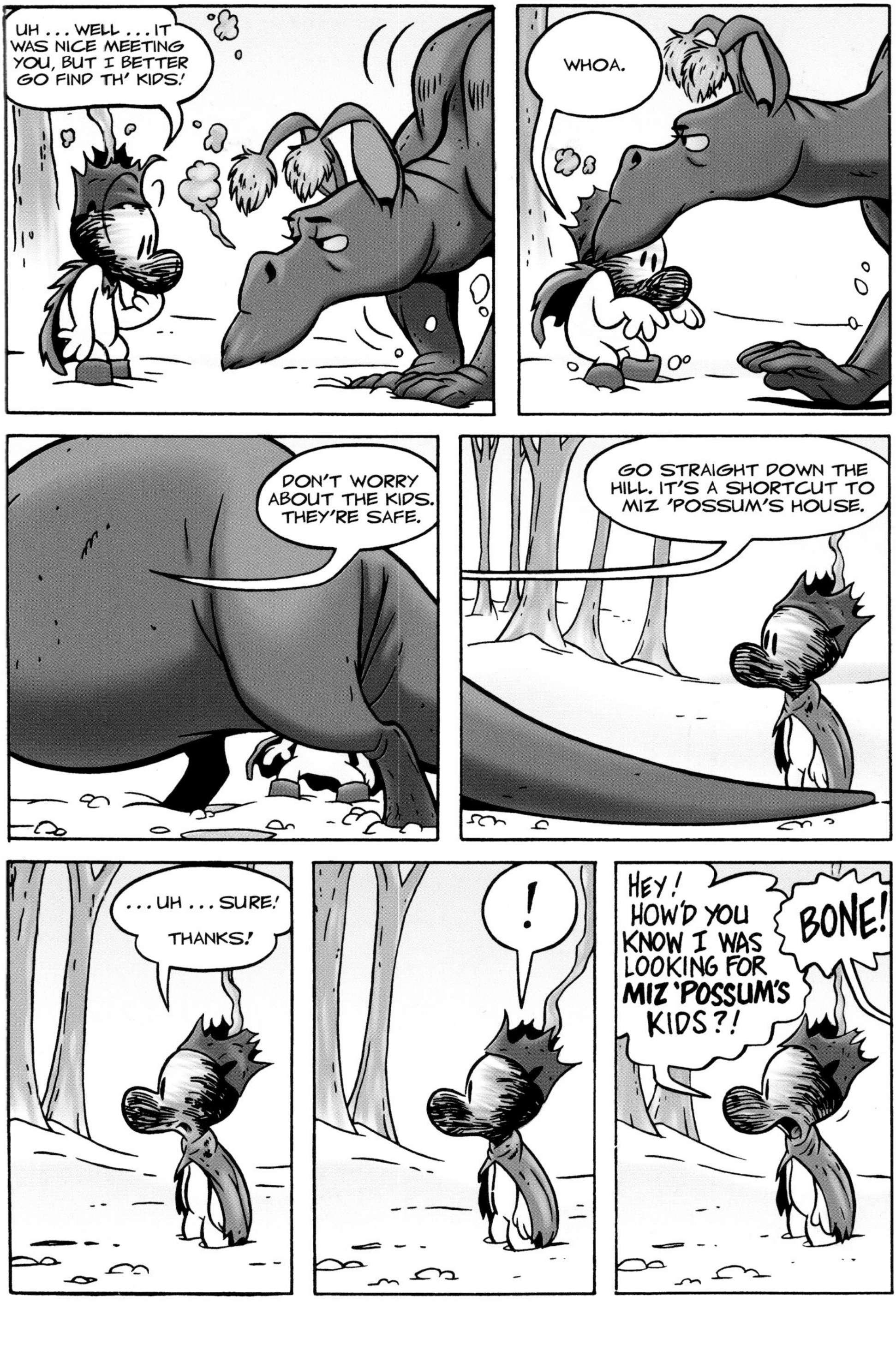
UH . . . WELL . . . IT WAS NICE MEETING YOU, BUT I BETTER GO FIND TH' KIDS!
WHOA.
DON'T WORRY ABOUT THE KIDS. THEY'RE SAFE.
GO STRAIGHT DOWN THE HILL. IT'S A SHORTCUT TO MIZ 'POSSUM'S HOUSE.
. . . UH . . . SURE!
THANKS!
!
HEY! HOW'D YOU KNOW I WAS LOOKING FOR MIZ 'POSSUM'S KIDS?!
BONE!

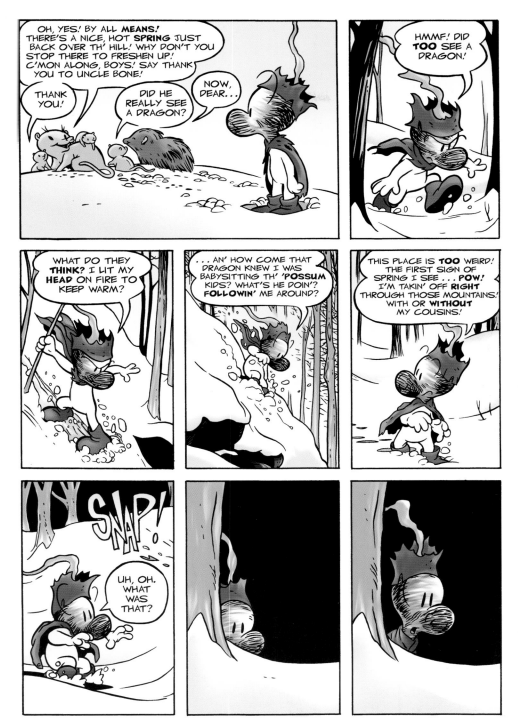

♪ MMMMMM ♪

FOOM!

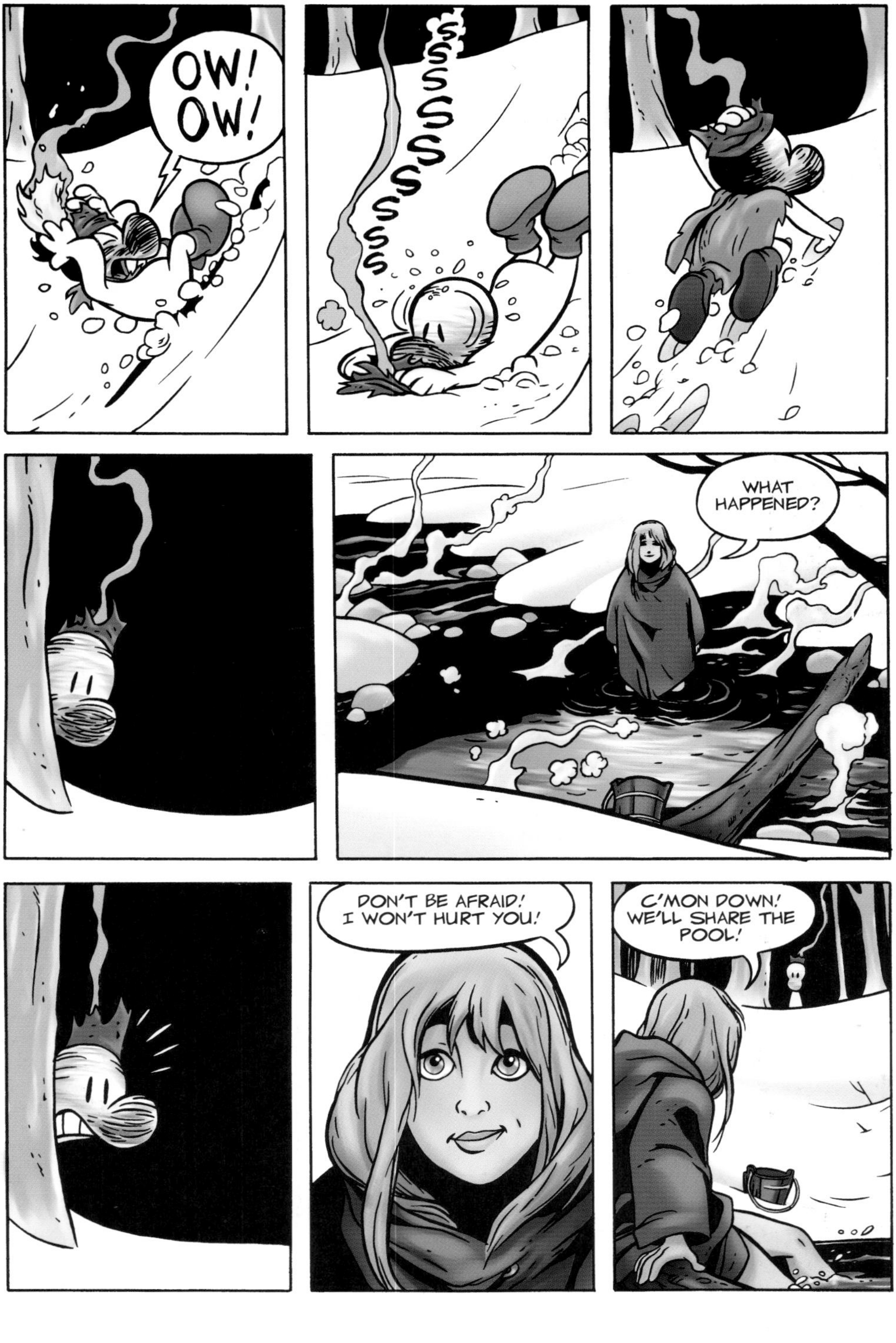
OW!
OW!
SSSSSSSSSSS
WHAT HAPPENED?
DON'T BE AFRAID! I WON'T HURT YOU!
C'MON DOWN! WE'LL SHARE THE POOL!

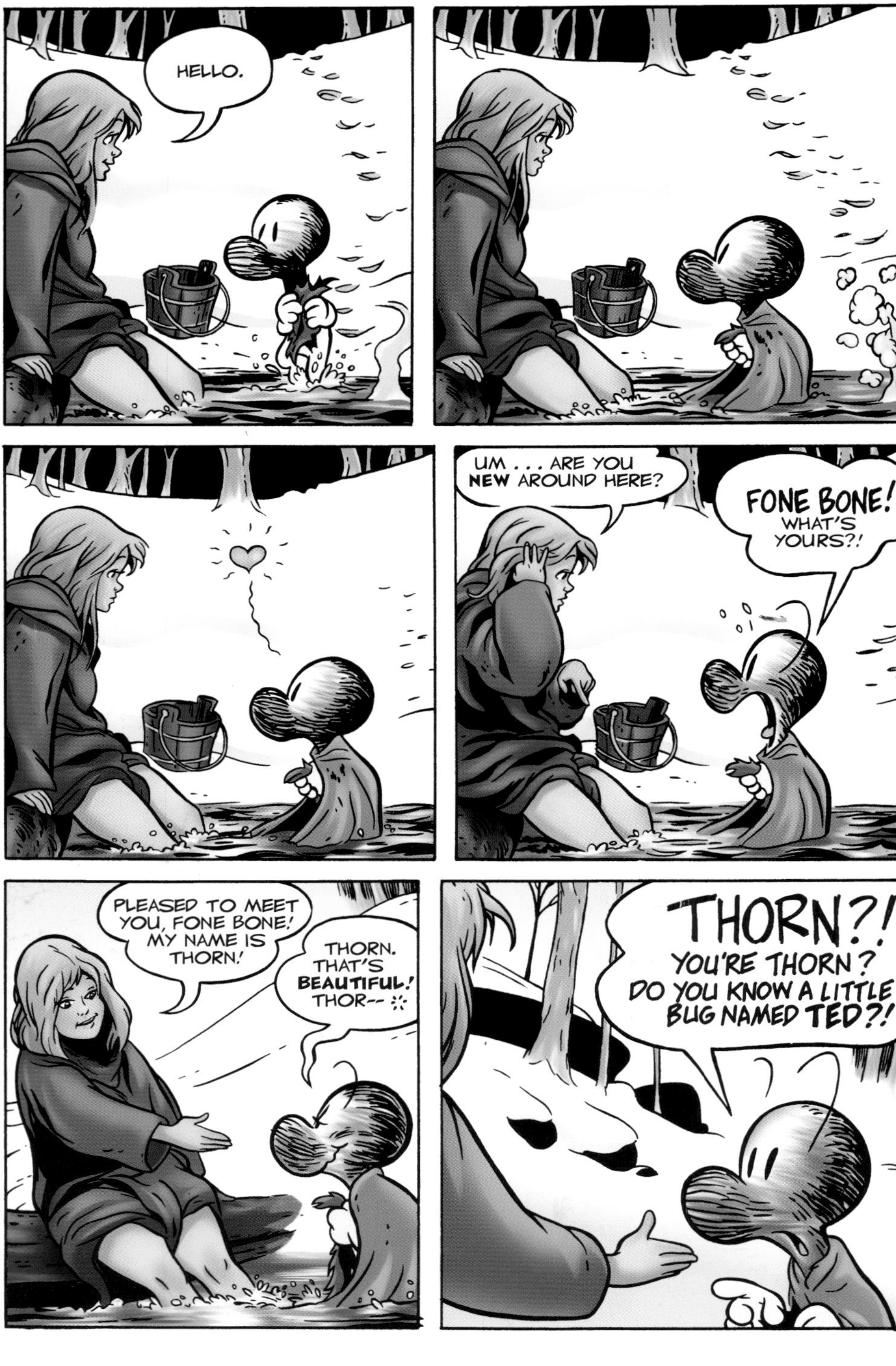
HELLO.
UM . . . ARE YOU NEW AROUND HERE?
FONE BONE! WHAT'S YOURS?!
PLEASED TO MEET YOU, FONE BONE! MY NAME IS THORN!
THORN. THAT'S BEAUTIFUL! THOR--
THORN?! YOU'RE THORN? DO YOU KNOW A LITTLE BUG NAMED TED?!

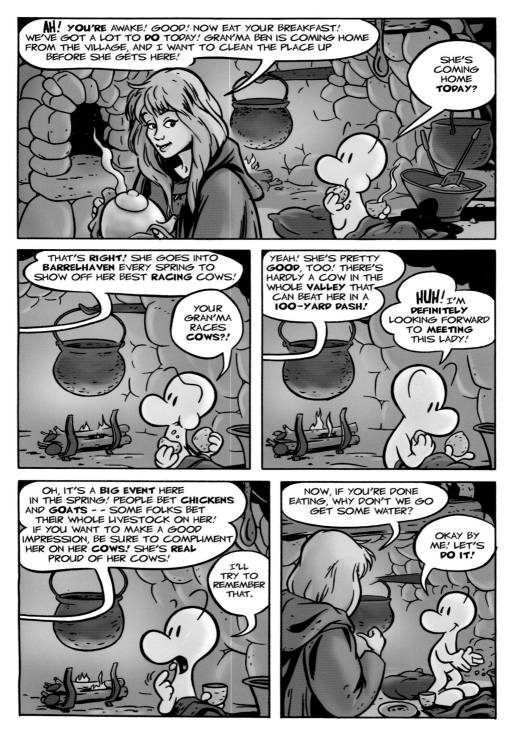

GRUMP! GRUMP! GRUMP!

GRUMP!

SPLOP

SPLOOOSH

OOOH! WAIT'LL I GET MY HANDS ON THAT COUSIN OF MINE!

I CAN'T **BELIEVE** FONE BONE WOULD JUST **LEAVE** ME OUT HERE WANDERING AROUND HELPLESS AND HUNGRY!

I'LL BET HE'S BACK IN BONEVILLE **RIGHT NOW.** SITTING IN **MY** HOUSE, EATING **MY** FOOD!

GLORP! RUMBLE! GRRRR

GROWL!

HEY! **SHUT UP!** I JUST ATE A **STICK** AN HOUR AGO! WHAT DO YOU **WANT** FROM ME?!

DO YOU LIKE APPLE PIE, FONE BONE?

LIKE IT? IT'S MY FAVORITE HOBBY!

WELL, DON'T GET TOO EXCITED!

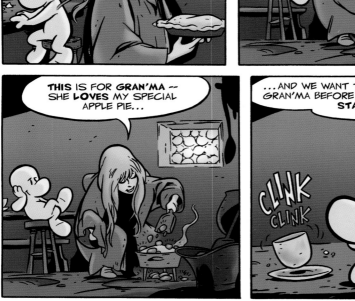

THIS IS FOR GRAN'MA -- SHE LOVES MY SPECIAL APPLE PIE...

...AND WE WANT TO BE REAL NICE TO GRAN'MA BEFORE WE ASK ABOUT YOU STAYING HERE!

CLINK CLINK

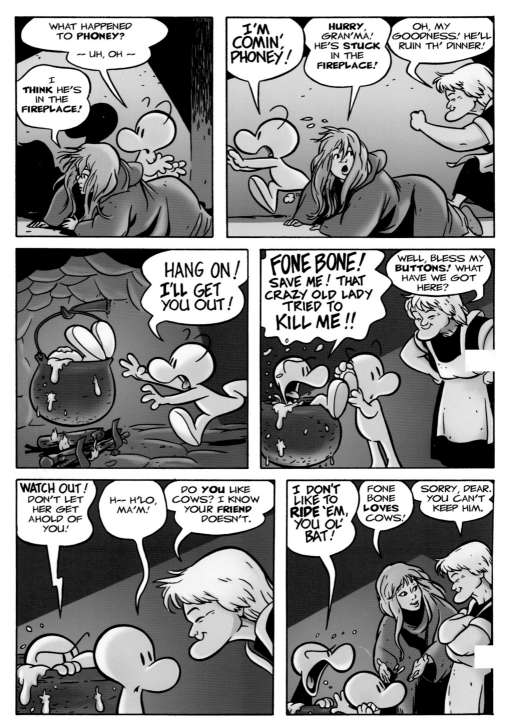

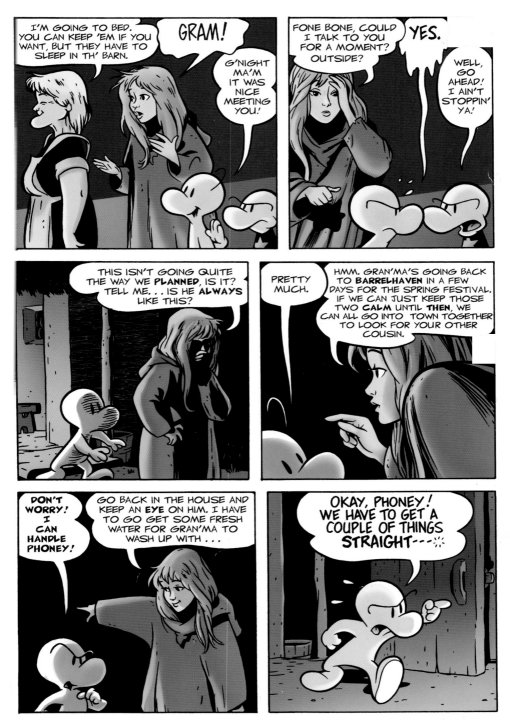

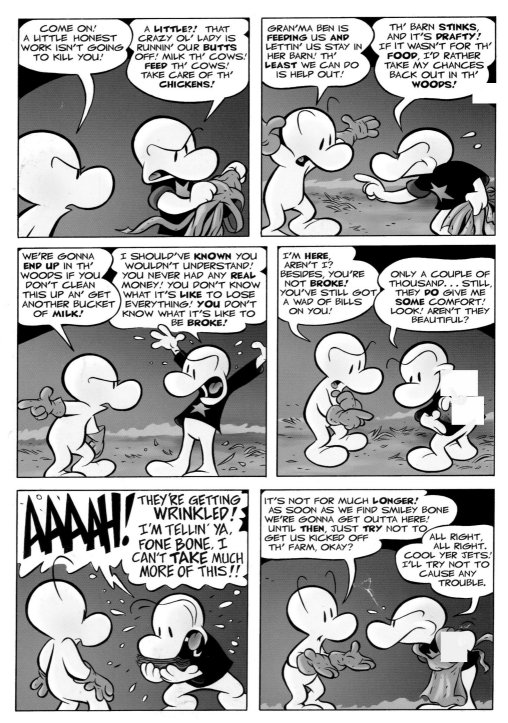

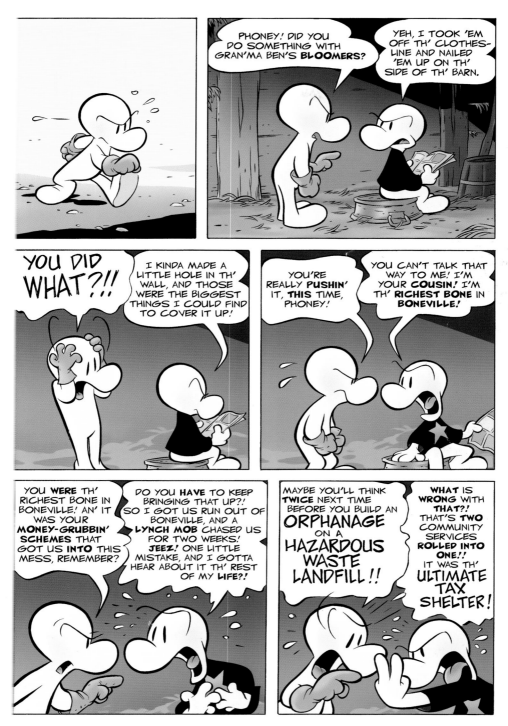

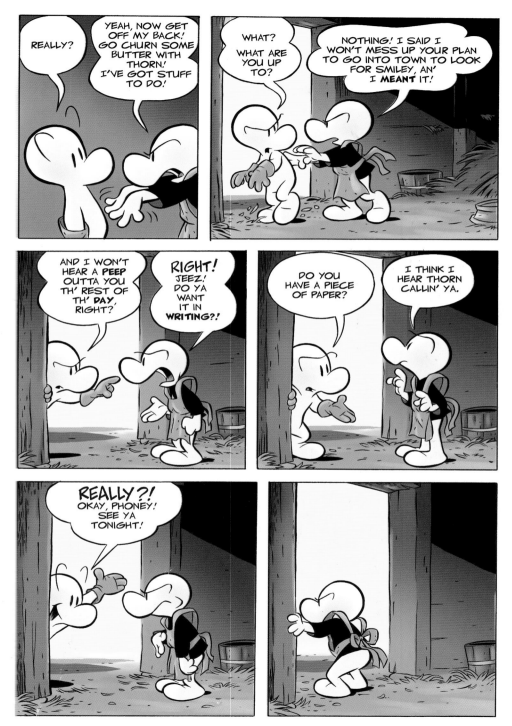

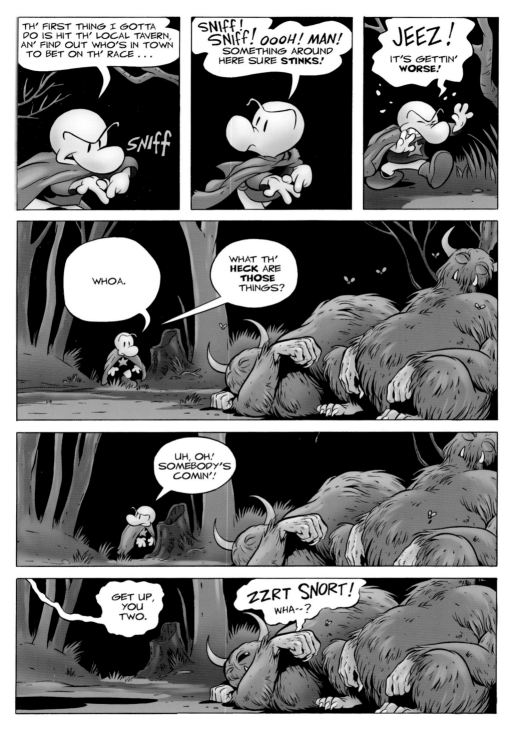

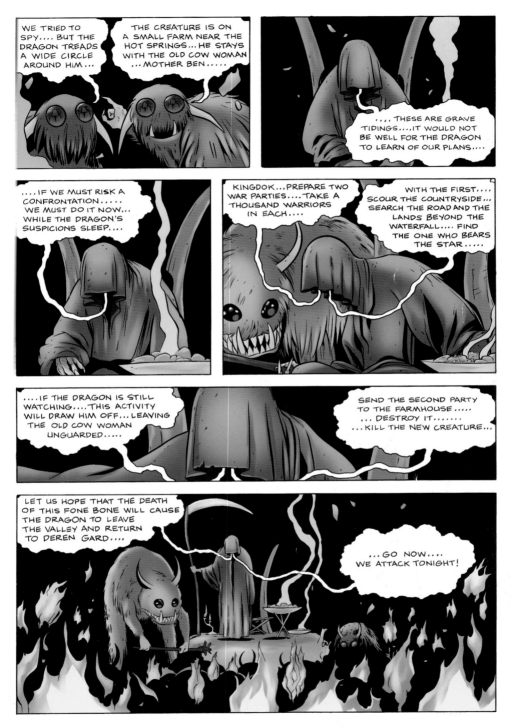

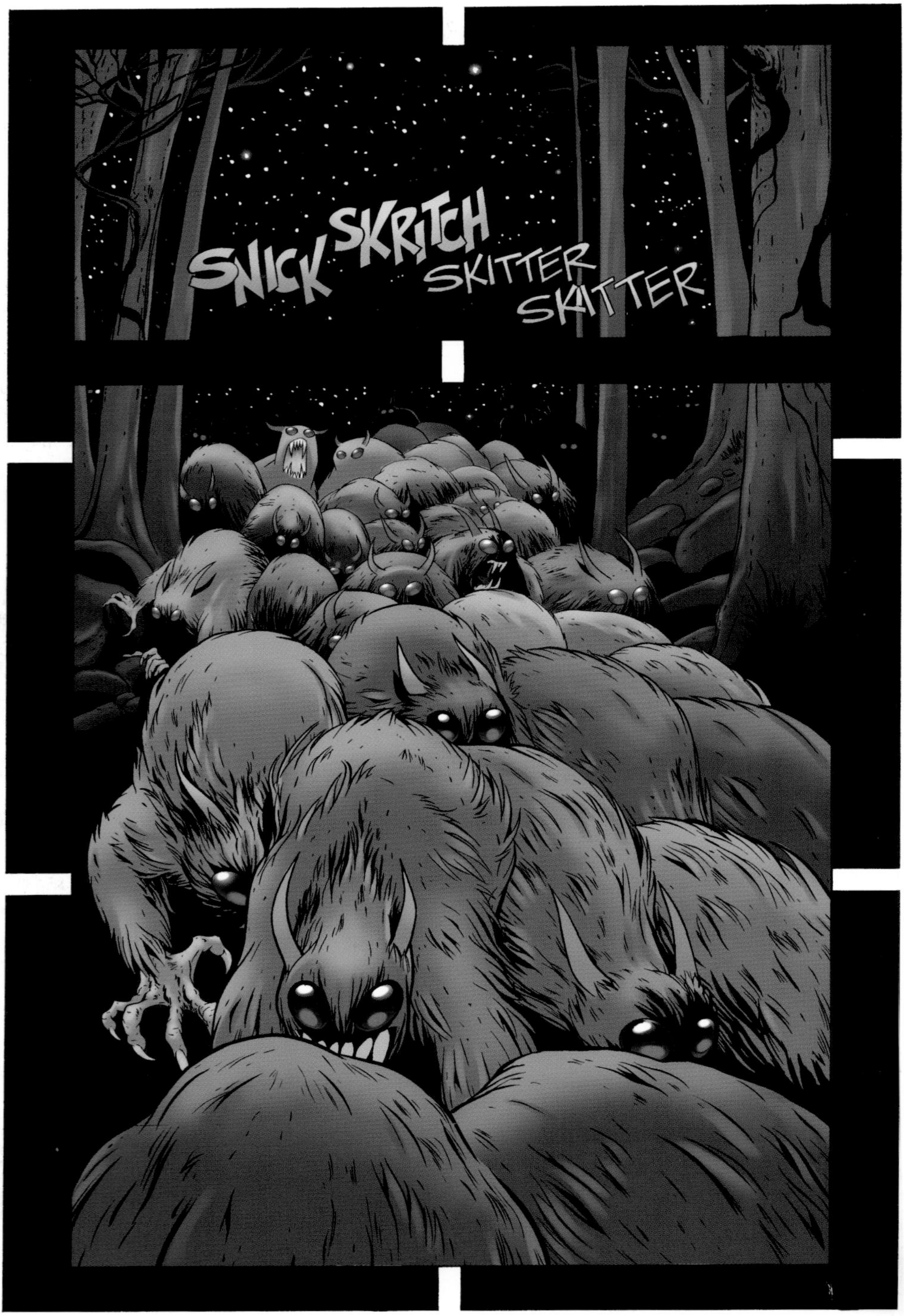
SNICK SKRITCH
SKITTER
SKITTER

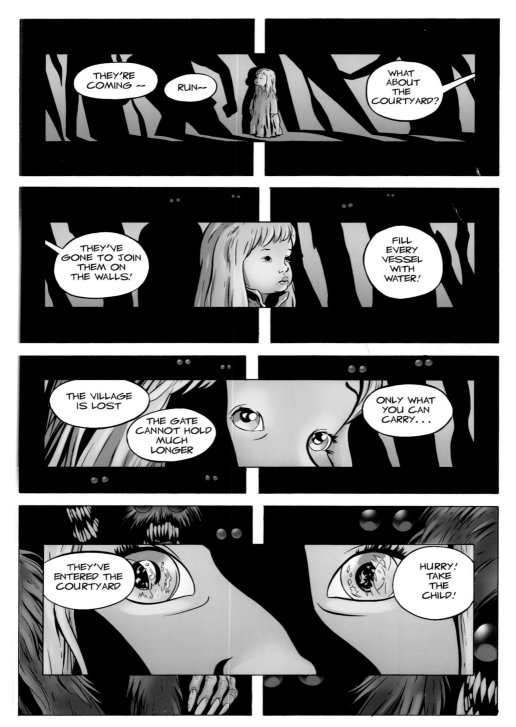

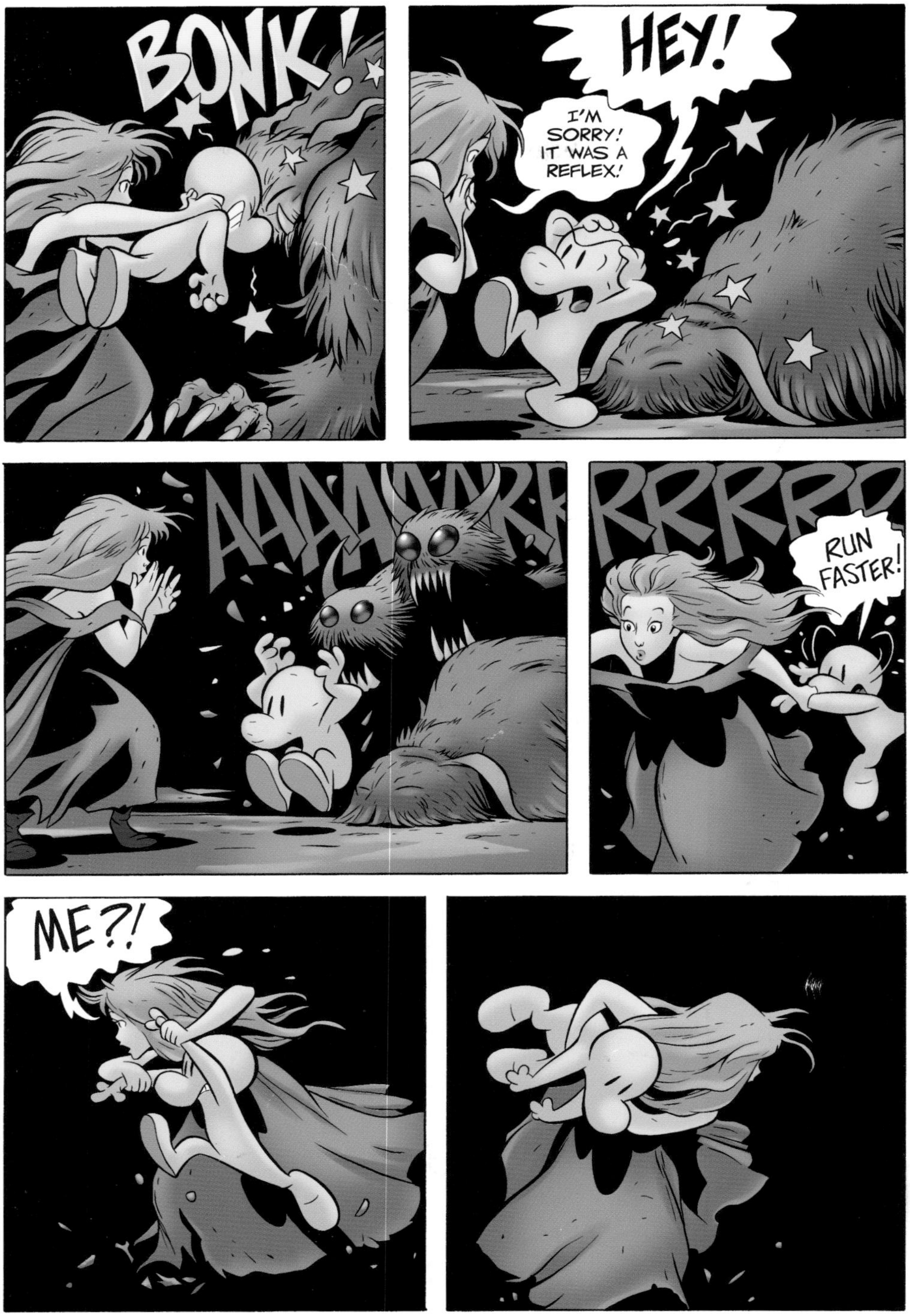
BONK!
HEY!
I'M SORRY! IT WAS A REFLEX!
AAAAARRRRRRR
RUN FASTER!
ME?!

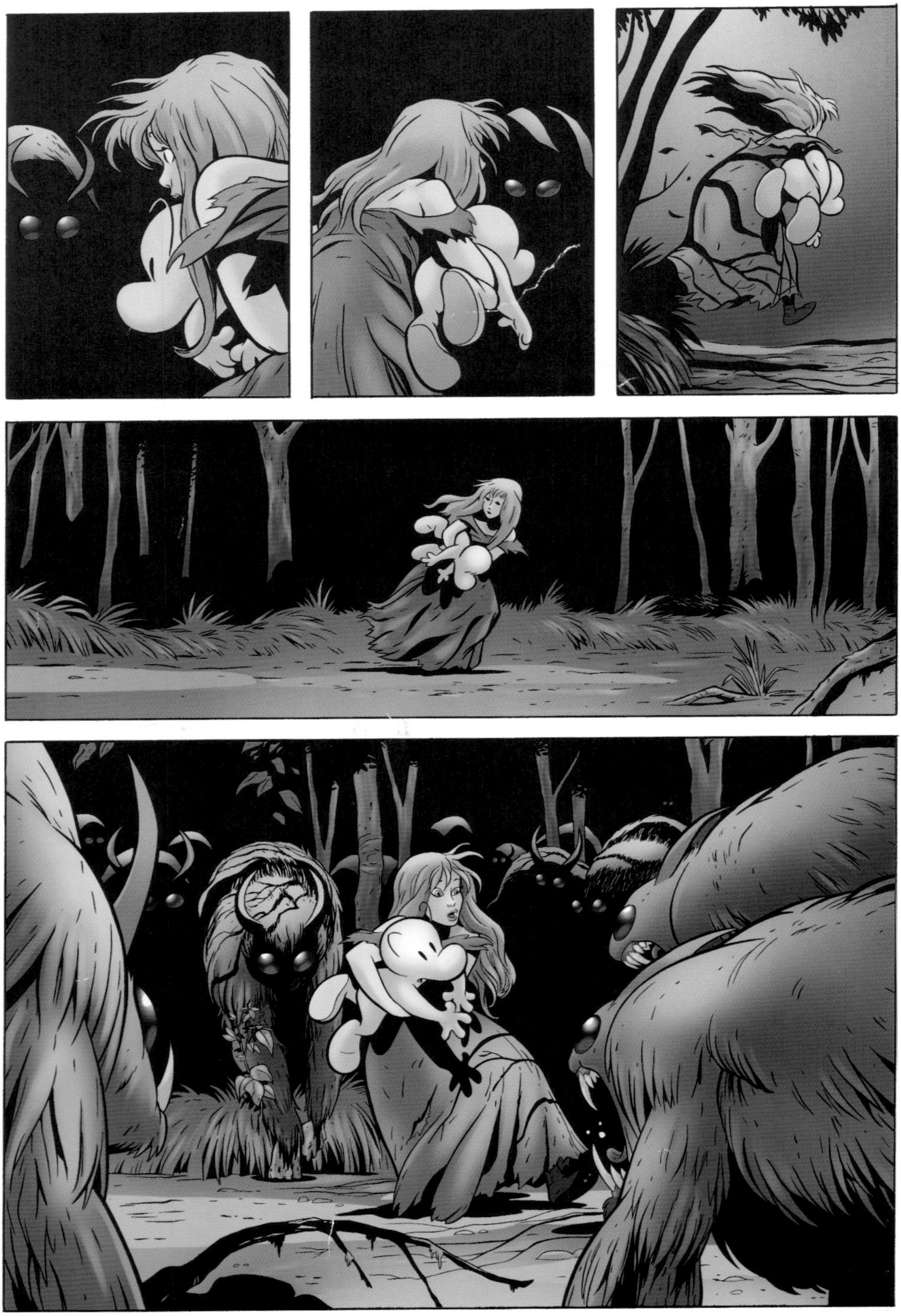

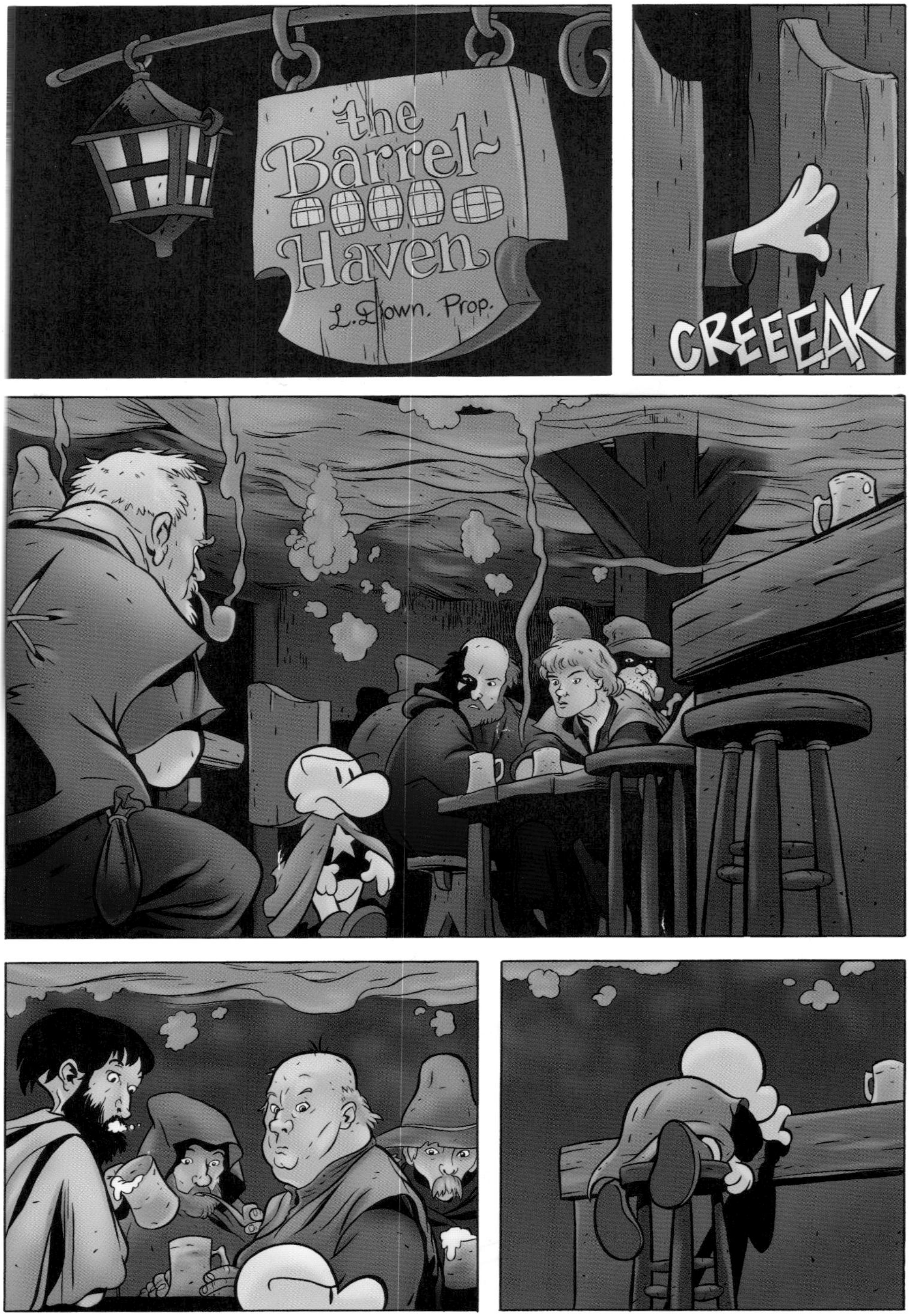
the Barrel Haven
L. Down. Prop.
CREEEAK

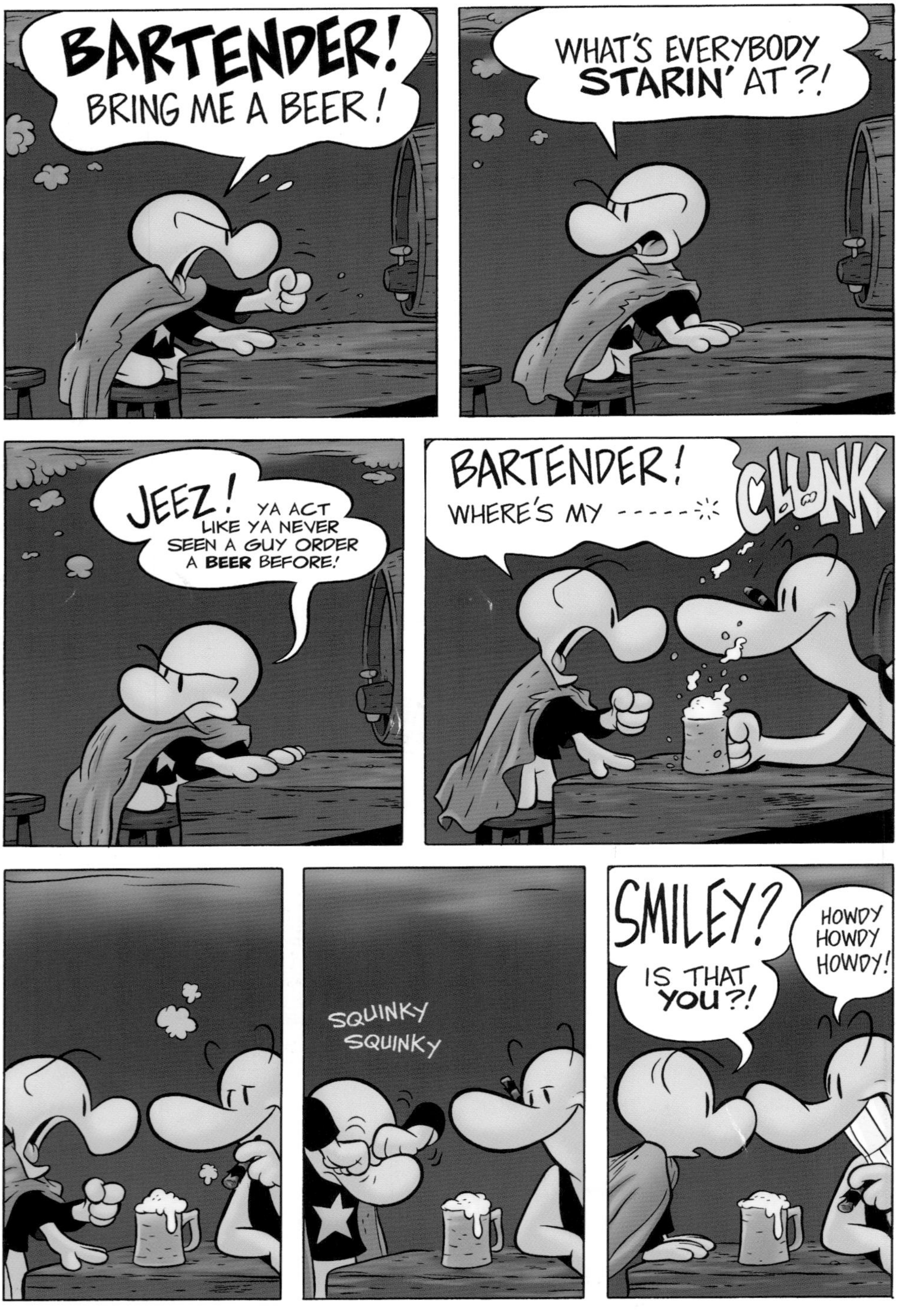
BARTENDER! BRING ME A BEER!
WHAT'S EVERYBODY STARIN' AT?!
JEEZ! YA ACT LIKE YA NEVER SEEN A GUY ORDER A BEER BEFORE!
BARTENDER! WHERE'S MY -----
CLUNK
SQUINKY SQUINKY
SMILEY? IS THAT YOU?!
HOWDY HOWDY HOWDY!

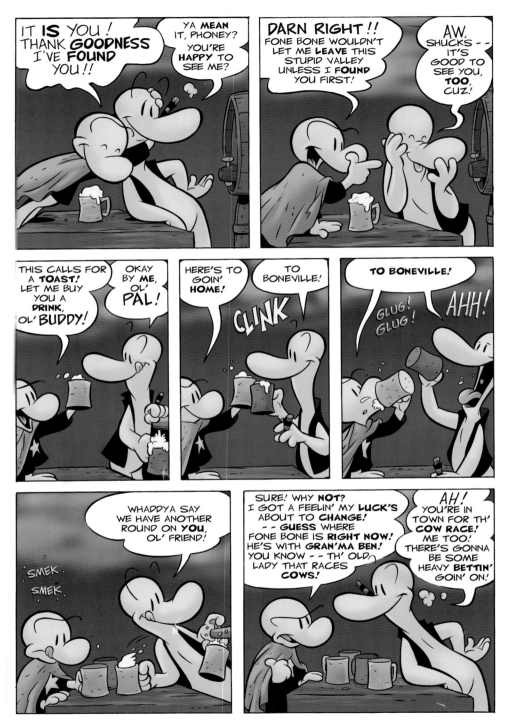

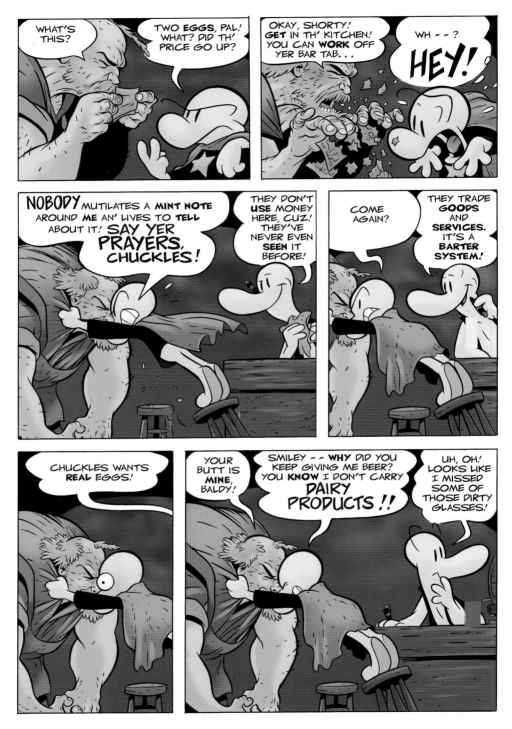

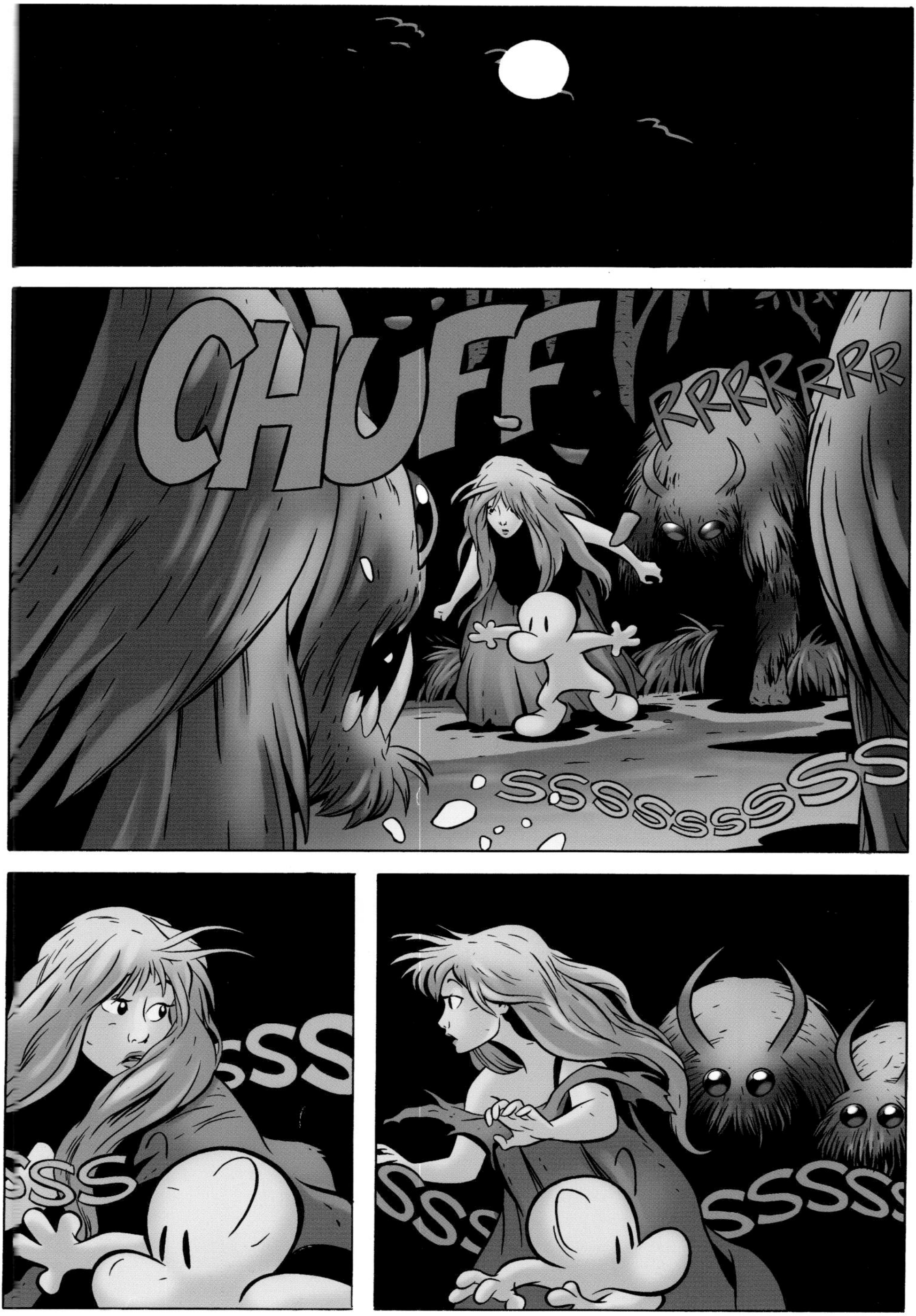
CHUFF
RRRRRRRR
SSSSSSSSSS
SSS
SSS
SSS
SSSSS

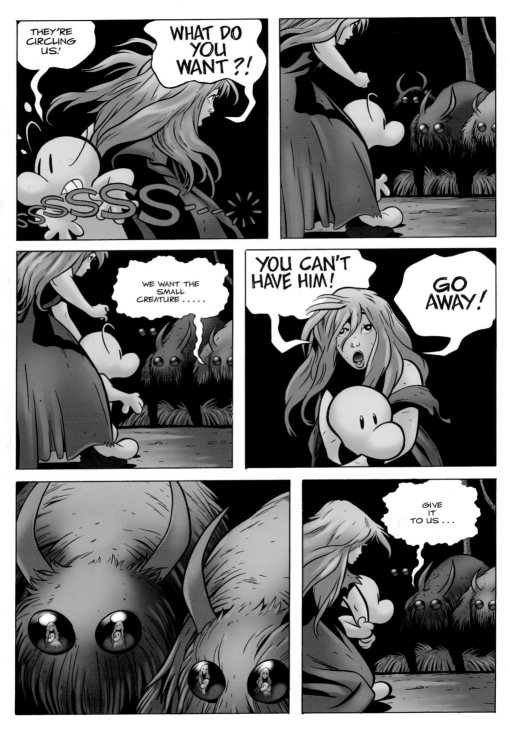

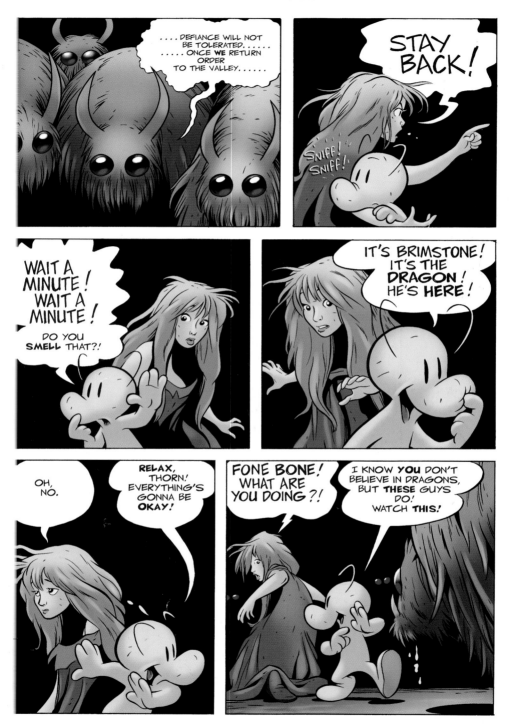

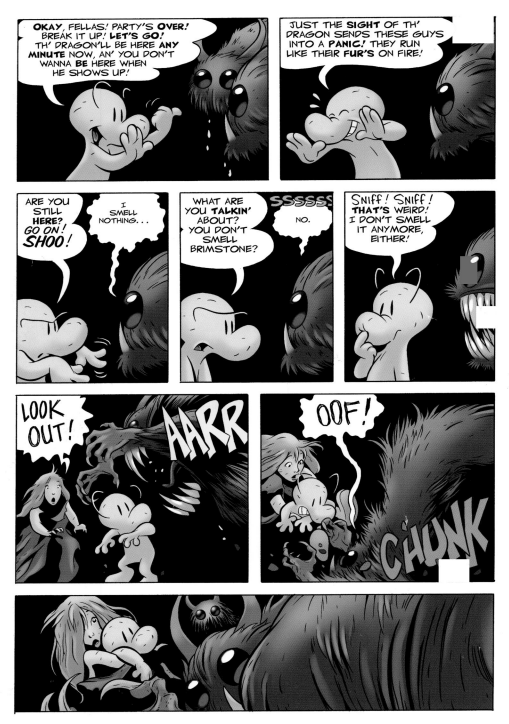

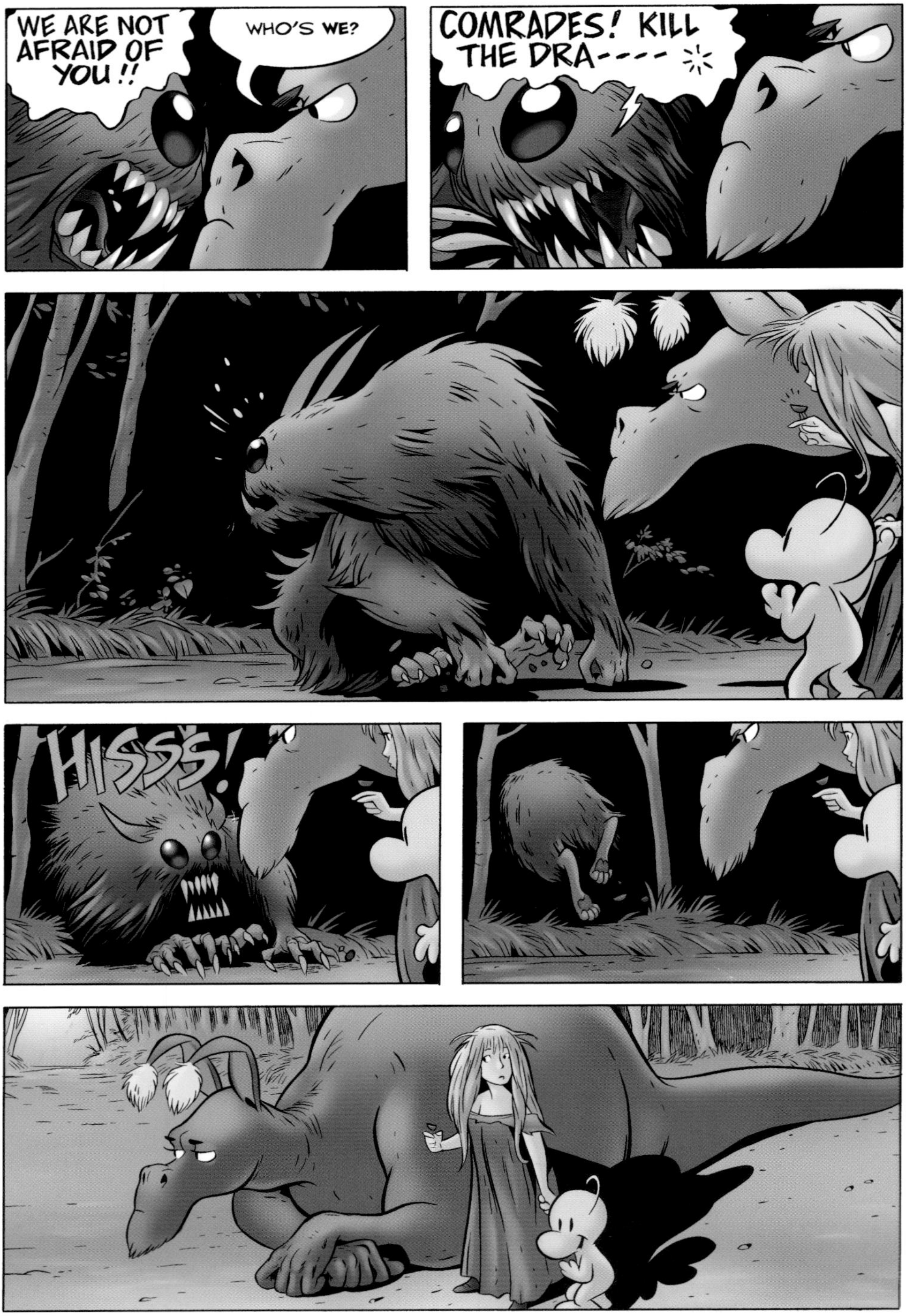
WE ARE NOT AFRAID OF YOU !!
WHO'S WE?
COMRADES! KILL THE DRA----
HISSS!

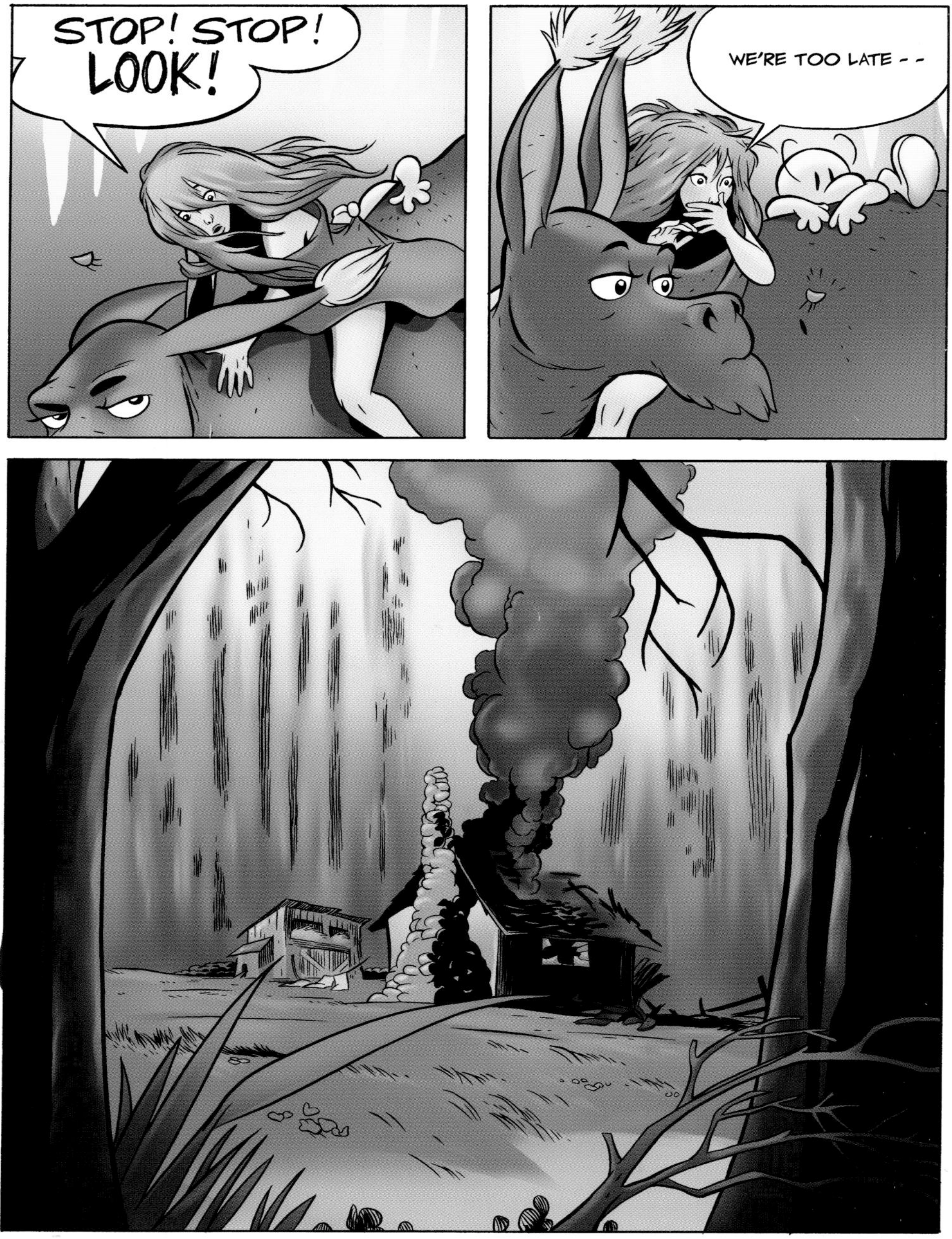
STOP! STOP! LOOK!
WE'RE TOO LATE - -

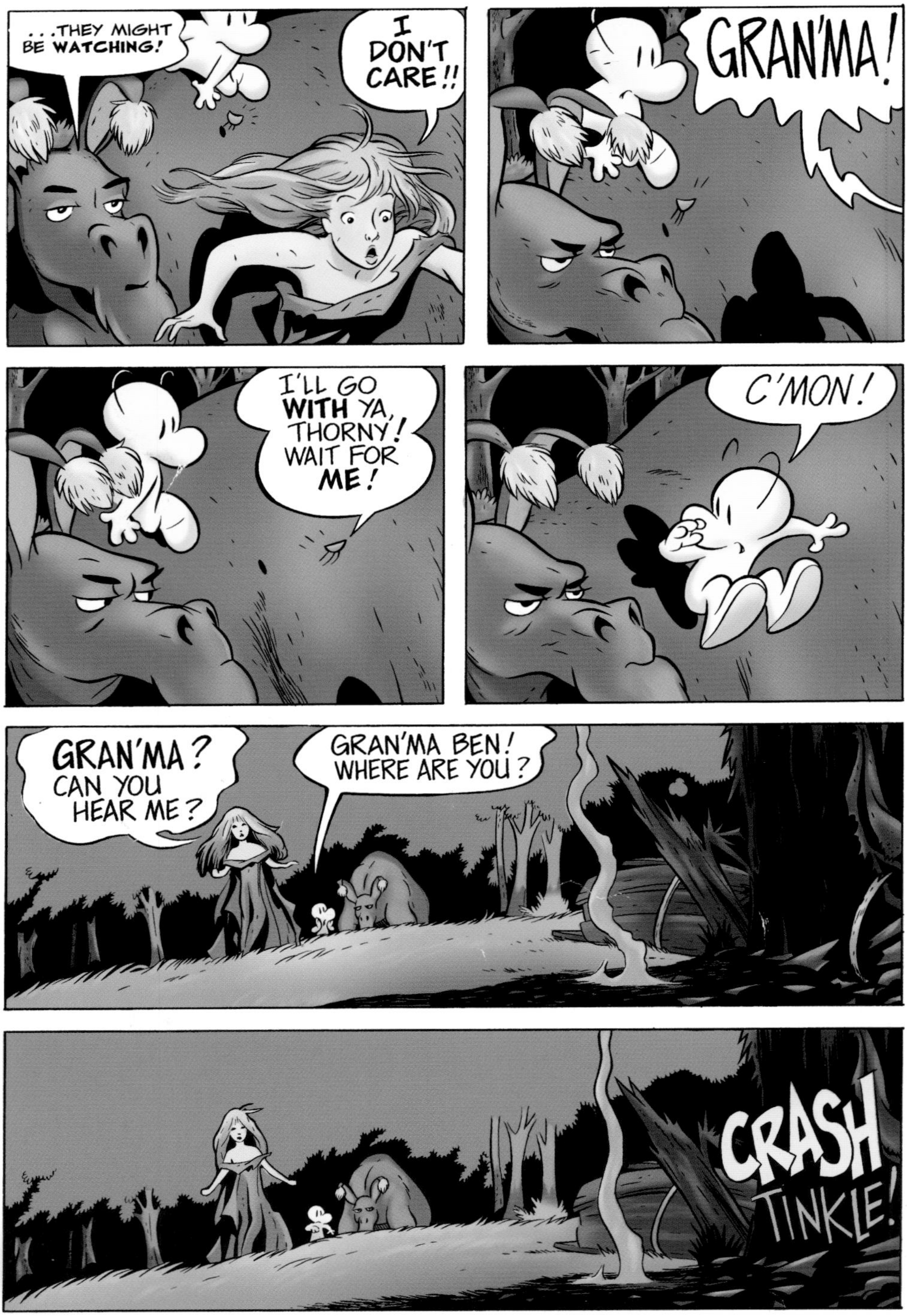
. . .THEY MIGHT BE WATCHING!
I DON'T CARE!!
GRAN'MA!
I'LL GO WITH YA, THORNY! WAIT FOR ME!
C'MON!
GRAN'MA? CAN YOU HEAR ME?
GRAN'MA BEN! WHERE ARE YOU?
CRASH
TINKLE!

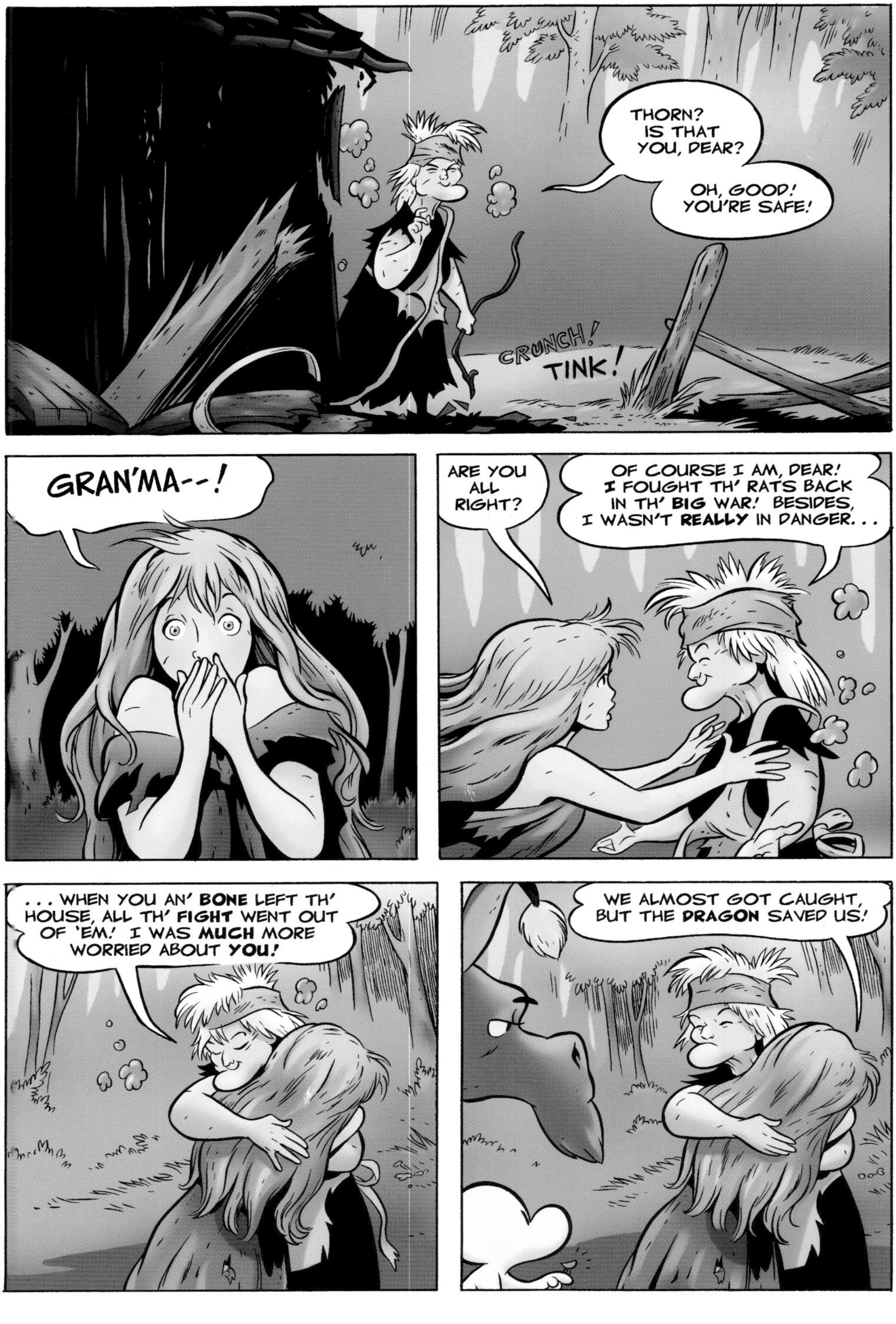
THORN? IS THAT YOU, DEAR?
OH, GOOD! YOU'RE SAFE!
CRUNCH!
TINK!
GRAN'MA--!
ARE YOU ALL RIGHT?
OF COURSE I AM, DEAR! I FOUGHT TH' RATS BACK IN TH' BIG WAR! BESIDES, I WASN'T REALLY IN DANGER...
...WHEN YOU AN' BONE LEFT TH' HOUSE, ALL TH' FIGHT WENT OUT OF 'EM! I WAS MUCH MORE WORRIED ABOUT YOU!
WE ALMOST GOT CAUGHT, BUT THE DRAGON SAVED US!

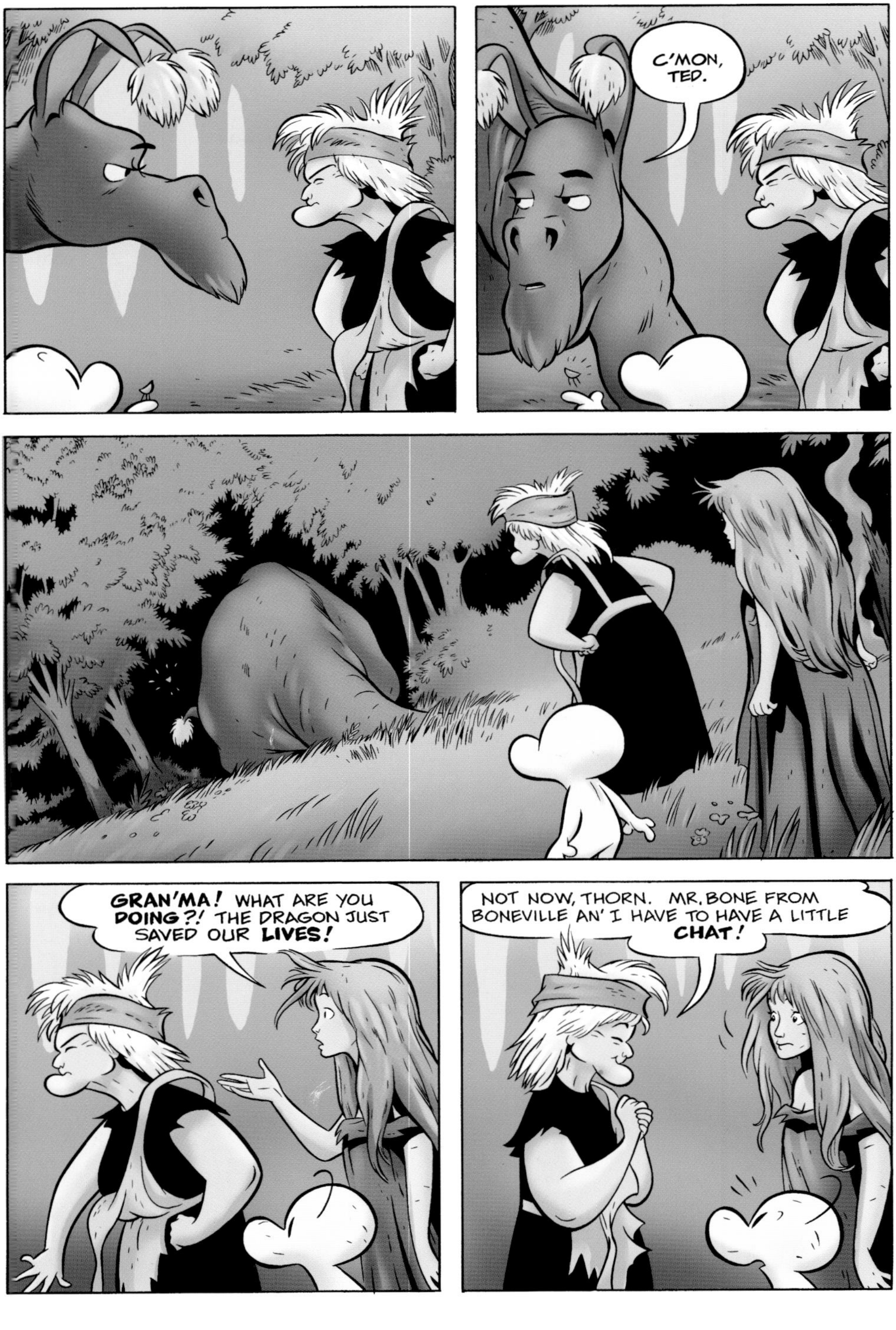
C'MON, TED.
GRAN'MA! WHAT ARE YOU DOING?! THE DRAGON JUST SAVED OUR LIVES!
NOT NOW, THORN. MR. BONE FROM BONEVILLE AN' I HAVE TO HAVE A LITTLE CHAT!

PHONEY INVITED **EVERYBODY** IN TOWN -- AN' HE PROMISED **FREE FOOD** FOR ANYONE WHO SHOWED UP! PRETTY SOON, TH' **PICNIC** WAS TH' **TALK** OF **BONEVILLE!**

THEN TH' BIG DAY ARRIVED, AN' TH' **WHOLE TOWN** TURNED OUT! TH' KIDS WERE PLAYIN' UNDER TH' TREES, AN' THE WOMEN WORE SUNBONNETS AN' FANCY DRESSES! THE PICNIC WAS OFF TO A **PERFECT START!**

THERE'S A **STATUE** IN TH' PARK OF BONEVILLE'S **FOUNDER** -- "**BIG**" JOHNSON BONE -- AN' SINCE MY COUSINS AN' I ARE **DESCENDANTS** OF HIS, PHONEY WANTED TO MAKE HIS ANNOUNCEMENT IN FRONT OF TH' STATUE.

. . . AND JUST TO **ADD** TO TH' FESTIVITIES, PHONEY HAD A **50** ft. **BALLOON** MADE OF HIMSELF! TH' BALLOON WAS TIED TO OL' "**BIG**" JOHNSON!

FASTEN THAT END THERE, WOULD YOU, BONE?

EVERYTHING WAS GOIN' **GREAT!** FOLKS WERE LISTENIN' TO TH' **FIREHOUSE** BAND AN' ENJOYIN' TH' SUNSHINE! TH' FOOD WAS PASSED OUT AN' THERE WERE PLENTY OF **PRUNE TARTS** FOR EVERYONE!

PRUNE TARTS?

YEAH. YOU KNOW PHONEY. HE GOT A GOOD DEAL ON SOME PRUNES FROM A DISCOUNT **PRUNE BROKER!**

OF COURSE!

HEY, **SMILEY**! TAKE THAT TUB OF GLASSES BACK TO YOUR BUDDY! WE'RE OUT OF **MUGS** AGAIN!

YES, **SIR**, MISTER DOWN!

HEY, THERE, PHONEY! LUCIUS SAYS YA GOTTA **WASH** THESE, **PRONTO**! WE GOT A LOT OF **THIRSTY** CUSTOMERS OUT FRONT!

OF COURSE, I MAKE **SURE** EVERYBODY GETS A **NEW**, **CLEAN** MUG WITH EACH DRINK!

YEAH. I NOTICED.

CLUNK

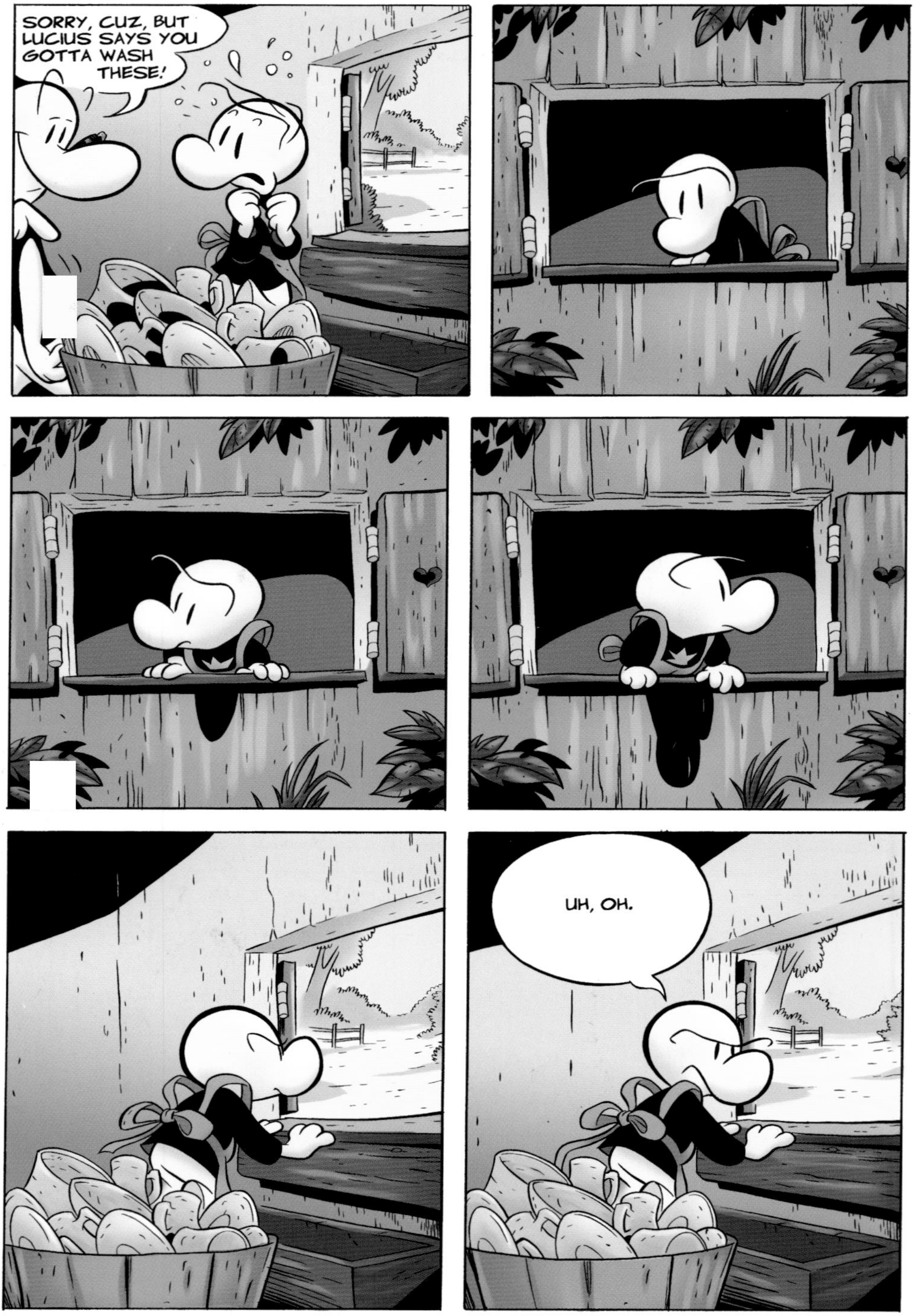
SORRY, CUZ, BUT LUCIUS SAYS YOU GOTTA WASH THESE!
UH, OH.

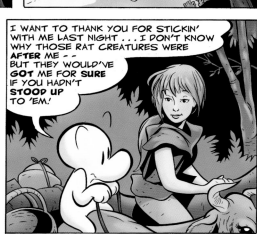

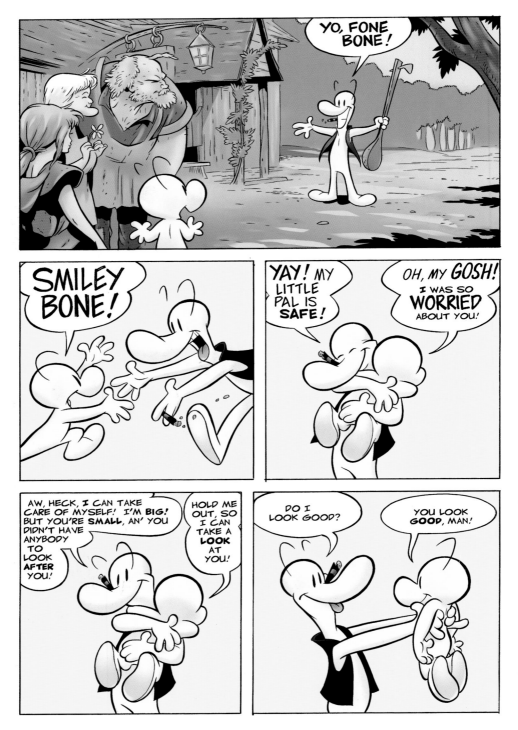

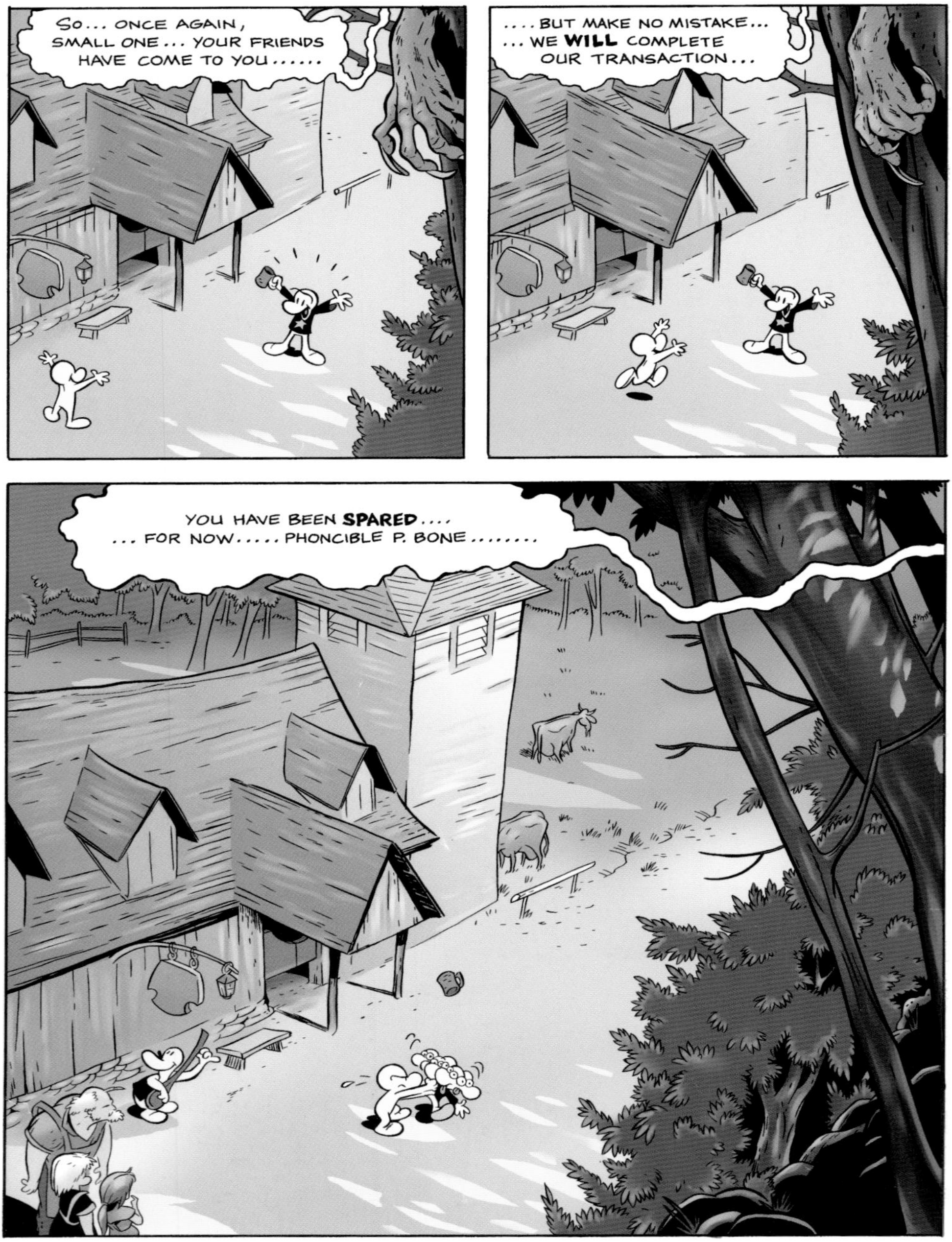
SO... ONCE AGAIN, SMALL ONE... YOUR FRIENDS HAVE COME TO YOU......
....BUT MAKE NO MISTAKE... ...WE **WILL** COMPLETE OUR TRANSACTION...
YOU HAVE BEEN **SPARED**.... ...FOR NOW..... PHONCIBLE P. BONE........

About JEFF SMITH

JEFF SMITH was born and raised in the American Midwest. He learned about cartooning from comic strips, comic books, and watching animated shorts on TV. After four years of drawing comic strips for Ohio State University's student newspaper and cofounding Character Builders animation studio in 1986, Smith launched the comic book *BONE* in 1991. Between *BONE* and other comics projects, Smith spends much of his time on the international guest circuit promoting comics and the art of graphic novels.

More about *BONE*

Instant classics when they first appeared in the U.S. as underground comic books in 1991, the *BONE* books have since garnered 38 international awards and sold a million copies in 15 languages. Now, Scholastic's GRAPHIX imprint is publishing full-color graphic novel editions of the nine-book *BONE* series. Look for the continuing adventures of the Bone cousins in *The Great Cow Race*.

Dreaming of Harvestar

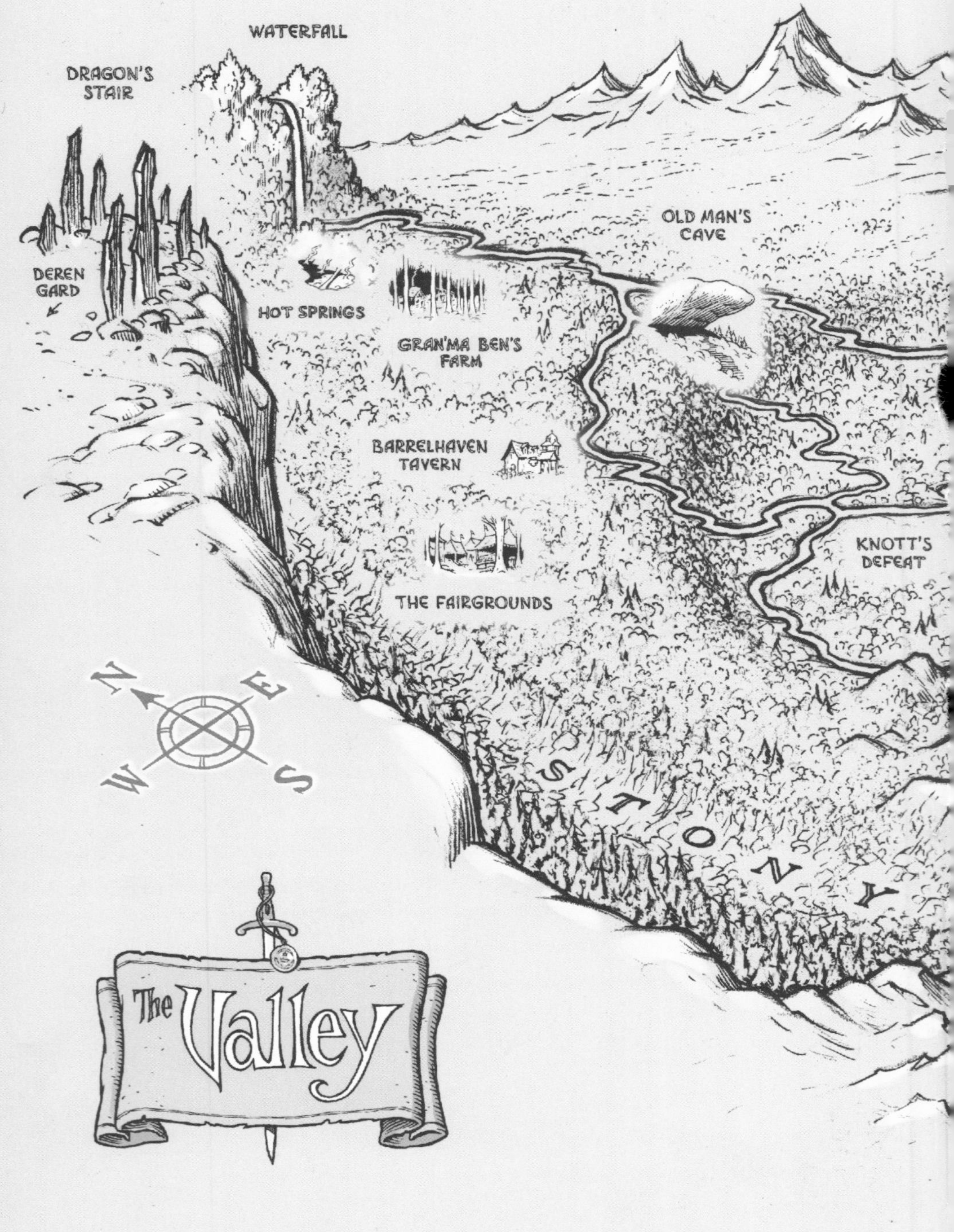
WATERFALL
DRAGON'S STAIR
DEREN GARD
HOT SPRINGS
OLD MAN'S CAVE
GRAN'MA BEN'S FARM
BARRELHAVEN TAVERN
THE FAIRGROUNDS
KNOTT'S DEFEAT
N
E
W
S
STONY
The Valley